For a long time Rebecca watched the stars, listening to the rumble and snort of the men who slept about the campfire.

Lantree also watched the stars, his head tipped so that she felt the tickle of his hair on her ear. After a while he turned his face and she watched his gaze settle on her.

She drew in a quick breath. The emotion she saw in his eyes was not that of a comfortable friend. He was a man wanting a woman… wanting *his* woman.

He touched her hair, smoothing back some of the tangles that the day's ride had caused.

"My sweet, beautiful Becca," he whispered.

There might be words in the universe to chastise that remark, but at that moment she could not find them…did not want to.

AUTHOR NOTE

Are you drawn to stories of the Old West like I am? There is something so unique about that time and place. It was a hard, rugged land that tested the mettle of those who ventured into it. At the same time it was a land of new beginnings. For some it was a place of refuge, where one could leave a regrettable past behind and start anew. For others, young and fresh with hope, it was a place to dig in roots and build a future. For many the Old West represented a way to throw off the constraints of proper society and live life on their own terms.

When Rebecca Louise Lane ventures to Montana it's for all three reasons. As destiny will, in the land of romance, it leads her to Lantree Boone Walker—a man who has gone West to hide from his past.

I hope you enjoy the story of how Rebecca and Lantree each find a new beginning, as well as a life together, in the wilds of Montana.

WED TO THE MONTANA COWBOY

Carol Arens

Published in Great Britain 2015
by Mills & Boon, an imprint of Harlequin (UK) Limited,
Eton House, 18-24 Paradise Road, Richmond, Surrey, TW9 1SR

© 2015 Carol Arens

ISBN: 978-0-263-24788-6

Harlequin (UK) Limited's policy is to use papers that are natural,
renewable and recyclable products and made from wood grown in
sustainable forests. The logging and manufacturing processes conform
to the legal environmental regulations of the country of origin.

Printed and bound in Spain
by CPI, Barcelona

Carol Arens delights in tossing fictional characters into hot water, watching them steam, and then giving them a happily-ever-after. When she's not writing she enjoys spending time with her family, beach-camping or lounging about a mountain cabin. At home, she enjoys playing with her grandchildren and gardening. During rare spare moments you will find her snuggled up with a good book.

Carol enjoys hearing from readers at carolarens@yahoo.com or on Facebook.

Books by Carol Arens

Mills & Boon® Historical Romance

Renegade Most Wanted
Rebel with a Cause
Christmas Cowboy Kisses
A Christmas Miracle
Rebel with a Heart
Wed to the Montana Cowboy

Linked by Character

Rebel Outlaw
Outlaw Hunter

Visit the author profile page at millsandboon.co.uk

Dedicated with love to the memory of Tony Arens.
Brother, we will always hear your boot-heels
two-stepping across our hearts.

Chapter One

◦◦◦◦◦◦◦◦◦◦

Kansas City, Missouri, April 1882

Despite appearances, Rebecca Lane was not a
wallflower.

Glancing to her left, then her right, she watched
her passed-over companions sitting primly against
the wall of the Kansas City Ladies Cultural Club
while the fiddler played his jumpy tune off-key.

While the other ladies might be considered
blushing flowers, waiting hopefully for some
man to pluck them from disgrace, she was not.

What she was, was a spinster.

If a man did come and pluck her, it would only
end in humiliation. There was no disguising the
fact that among the dainty wallflowers wilting in
their chairs she stood out as bold as a ragweed.

If this were not a charity event, and if Aunt
Eunice had not spent the best part of an hour

casting frowns at her, she would stand tall, very tall, six feet worth of tall to be exact, and escape this hall of merry, dancing people.

A sigh coming from her right reminded her that not everyone was merry. If she had an ounce of spit, she'd unite her sisters in humiliation and together they would march out the door.

Perhaps not Mary Crowner, though. Willard Phipp had just lifted her from her seat of misery and whirled her onto the dance floor.

Because Rebecca had idle moments with nothing to do but tap her toe and clench her fingers together, she considered her future.

There were a few fates worse than being a spinster, and truth be told, some advantages. She closed her eyes to the colorful skirts twirling past her feet. As she often did, she recited the advantages in her mind.

One, no man would tell her what to say. Two, no man would tell her what to wear. Three, no man would dictate where she could go or when she could go there.

But—and she never made it through the advantages before this thought sneaked in—no man would ever tell her that he loved her.

"Rebecca Louise Lane," her aunt's voice

hissed in her ear. "Why must you sit so tall? Your head is bobbing above the rest."

Was her head bobbing? No, certainly her aunt had made that up.

"How do you expect to ever get a husband?"

She didn't, of course, but to say so out loud would put the woman who had raised her in a foul mood, so she shrugged instead.

"Now, slouch down…and for heaven's sake, smile. I just saw Randall Pile looking your way."

"Yes, Aunt Eunice." She slid her posterior forward on the chair so that her shoulders sunk to the level of the girl sitting beside her.

Sadly, this position jutted her knees out and made her look… Well, she wouldn't think about that. She only hoped that no one tripped over them.

She peered through the throng of bobbing, whirling dancers, searching for Randall. Please, oh, please let her aunt have been mistaken about the fellow's interest in her.

Randall, in his boots, was five feet tall.

A yellow skirt whipped out of her line of vision and there he was, staring at her. Not at Martha on her right…not at Lucy on her left, but smack, square at her.

He was with a group of young men. One of

them elbowed him in the side. Another whispered in his ear. Randall laughed…well, smirked more like it.

This could only end in a way that would not please Aunt Eunice.

Martha's shame was suddenly lifted when a young man asked her to dance.

A flash of lavender ruffle settled into the empty chair beside Rebecca.

"Becca, sit up straight." Winded, her cousin Melinda frowned at her and yanked her elbow. "You are far too beautiful to be scrunched up like that."

Melinda was a lively, pretty girl who rarely went without a dance partner. The one whom she had apparently abandoned in the middle of a quickstep stood alone in the revelry looking bewildered.

"I saw Mama talking to you. Don't pay a whit of attention to whatever she had to say."

Rebecca sat up and took a long, shuddering breath.

"If only I could. She's set on matching me up with Randall again."

"I can't imagine what Mama is thinking. Randall Pile is—"

"Walking this way," Rebecca groaned.

"If we hurry we can escape outside before he makes it across the room."

For pity's sake, the man was fast. She hadn't taken three steps from her chair before he stood before her, chest puffed and looking arrogant to his boot toe.

"Would you care to dance, Miss Lane?"

By George she would not! Sadly, the interested gazes of several people in the room turned her way. She did not wish to make a scene.

Melinda's abandoned dance partner appeared out of the crowd. "Miss Winston, may I have the pleasure...again?"

"Billy!" Melinda exclaimed. "How beastly of me to leave you the way I did. I'd be delighted to continue."

Clearly Billy held no grudge. A grin split his face, as cheerful as the bright quarter moon visible through the window.

Randall grinned as well, but it was over his shoulder at his companions, not at any pleasure over dancing with her. No doubt he had made the offer on a dare...possibly money had changed hands.

One of the wallflowers giggled. And why would she not? She and Randall must look like a giraffe and a peacock engaged in some bizarre ritual.

She would give her aunt this one satisfaction, then beg some indisposition and go home.

A slow walk around Palmer's cornfield with the brisk night air brushing her cheeks would cleanse away the humiliation as effectively as a classical melody would.

The fiddler played a twisted version of a polka. Did no one else hear the off-key screech that felt like pinpricks inside one's bones?

She glanced about.

Apparently not. Everyone seemed to be having a fine high time.

Randall, more than most. He stomped on her skirt with every turn. His clutching, sweaty hand was bound to leave a stain on her dress.

Exasperated, she glared down at the top of his head, noticing that his hair was thinning. She had the urge to blow a fleck of dandruff from his scalp.

She might have made all sorts of inappropriate faces at him for all he would notice.

The one and only thing the man cared to look at was her bosom. And not because it was anything more than adequate but because unless he looked up or down, it's where his gaze fell.

His nose began to twitch…and sniff. He licked his lips, then for the first time he looked into her eyes…arched one brow.

Why, the little maggot!

She shoved him away. That ought to have been the end of it but he said, "I thought you'd be grateful."

So, when he turned to walk back to his snickering friends she raised her skirt to her knee, lifted her boot and kicked him hard in the rump.

Sadly for Aunt Eunice's reputation, which her aunt valued above anything, Randall lost his balance and skidded belly-first across the floor.

Everyone noticed.

In the chaos that followed, Melinda grabbed her hand. Together, they fled out the front door, down the steps and into the night.

The moment of reckoning came at one minute past midnight, even though Aunt Eunice had arrived home an hour after the unfortunate event.

Summoned, Rebecca stood before her aunt with her head bowed and her hands folded in front of her. She had taken this position many times over the years. The only difference between now and then was that when she was four years old, she had to look up into her aunt's scowl…now she looked down at it.

"Kindly explain why you would do such a thing…humiliate me and your poor cousins so horribly."

Melinda, clearly, had not been humiliated, but Bethune and Prudence were no doubt sobbing their mortification into their pillows at this moment.

"I never meant to—"

"It's Becca who was humiliated, Mama." All of a sudden, her defender stood beside her. "That horrible little man—"

"Might have been willing to offer for her hand, given his own limitations."

"Any man would be lucky to have our Becca!"

"Go to your room, Melinda," her aunt declared drily.

Melinda was far too old to be told to go to her room, just as Rebecca was far too old to be taking this scolding. But by George, no one wanted to send Eunice into a temper that might go on for days.

So, Melinda went to her room while Rebecca slouched another two inches.

Aunt Eunice had been distressed over Rebecca's height since the day she had been dropped on her doorstep. At four years old she had towered over Bethune who was five and a half.

"Do you want to be an old maid, Rebecca?" Aunt Eunice arched one eyebrow. "Or worse... have people wonder if you grew up to be like your mother...that I allowed you to?"

It would be difficult to know whether she committed the great sin of growing up like her mother or not. The memories of her life before coming to live with Aunt Eunice were vague.

She did recall the scent of rose water, and a fairy-like woman who laughed out loud but cried even louder. There was always a blur of men's faces in her memory. Sometimes she thought her mother's tears had to do with them.

But just as often she wondered if it was her that had made Mama weep because she was not pretty enough to make Papa stay.

It had been the dolls that made her think that. Mama carried a collection of blue-eyed princesses to whichever place they happened to be living. Papa had bought them for her, Mama liked to say, because they reminded him of her. Back then, they reminded Rebecca of angels. Later on when she thought of those pretty porcelain gifts, it hurt dreadfully.

In all their travels, Mama had never left a

doll behind. She'd left Rebecca behind without a backward glance.

"I have accepted the fact that I will, in all likelihood, remain unmarried." It stung that her aunt continued to fear that she would suddenly become promiscuous. "But I am nothing like my mother and have gone to great pains to show that I am not."

"As this evening would attest? Really, Rebecca, I've done my best with you but sometimes I fear that no matter how strict I am, you rebel… You are my sister all over again."

Whether that was true or not, she couldn't say. Mama had become a distant memory, buried so deep that trying to recall her face was like painting with mist.

"Aunt Eunice, the mother I remember is you." A woman who hid rare, tender feelings behind a starchy demeanor. She could only recall one instance when her aunt had showed her unguarded affection. When she was six years old, Rebecca had been seriously ill with a fever and her aunt had sat up with her for two days and nights, wiping her brow and crooning lullabies. During the worst of it she had even called her Becca.

"I regret that I shamed you, but Randall was

behaving like a lewd goat. I merely defended myself."

"And as usual, you dragged my Melinda into the mess."

Anyone acquainted with her cousin for more than ten minutes knew that there was no dragging Melinda. She dove into life headlong, laughing while she did so.

The clock on the fireplace mantel ticked off long silent seconds while her aunt stared up at her.

"You need a husband," she declared at last. "I hoped it would be Randall since you are of an age. But after tonight that is unlikely. But mark my words, Rebecca Louise, you will marry and marry soon."

Aunt Eunice sighed loudly, glanced at the clock then back up at her.

"Mr. Fielding, the butcher, has asked for you. He believes that with your size, you will be helpful in the shop. Count your blessings, young lady, that the man wants a hefty girl."

Hefty? Why, she was no such thing. She was slender, and if not delicate, exactly, she was by no means strapping.

"You may go to your room now."

There were many things that she would do

to keep peace with her aunt. After all, she did owe her a great deal. A widow after only five years of marriage, she had managed to raise four girls all on her own. She truly did deserve respect for that.

But showing her aunt respect stopped a good deal short of marrying the butcher.

"Rebecca." Her aunt's voice caught her just as she made the turn from the parlor to the hall. "As horrified as I am at how you behaved tonight, I'm glad that you did not let that pitiful Randall make improper advances. Once you are under the butcher's care, you'll be safe from that sort of conduct."

"Yes, Aunt Eunice," she said, but it was the last thing she meant.

A footpath crossed the backyard then sloped downhill toward the creek behind the house. Rebecca followed the trail of daffodils growing beside it, watching them nod their pretty yellow heads in the glow of the low-hung moon.

It was dark in the wee hours, but that didn't mean the flowers did not continue to flash their color. She decided to be like those bold little beauties…shine even during the dark hours.

Sitting on a bench that she had placed beside

the creek three years ago, she drew her violin from its case and began to play.

As the sound filtered through the cottonwoods, her nerves began to settle. With each draw of the bow across the strings, despair melted...hope took its place.

After a few moments she was smiling. The instrument always had this effect upon her. Learning to play it had come naturally.

"Do not, under any circumstances, marry the butcher." Melinda plopped down beside her, out of breath. She must have run all the way from the house. "I'm certain his first two wives were perfectly miserable."

Melinda, her fair hair loose and tumbling, her nightshift a soft white glow in the dark, was everything lovely. Her lively, engaging spirit had a way of drawing people to her. If she decided to postpone marriage for years, she would still be snatched up in a heartbeat. Her cousin might live to be a hundred years old and still not be considered an old maid.

"Your mother can be very determined."

"But not as determined as us... You wouldn't consider it? Please say you wouldn't!"

Rebecca placed her violin in its case then cradled it across her knees.

"I would not, not in a million years."

What was she going to do, though? Become a lifelong burden to her aunt? Eventually, when they were both old, become her caregiver?

A few hours ago, any slim hope of finding a decent man had slid across the floor of the social room with Randall Pile. No doubt the gentlemen of Kansas City were shaking their heads in astonishment. Perhaps even the butcher was having second thoughts.

"But there is something I've been considering for some time now." She paused and drew a breath. "I'll go to my grandfather."

"You can't do that, Becca! He lives in the wilderness with bears and wolves! Your home is here with us."

"I only live here. This is your home, your sisters' and your mother's. There's no future for me here."

"When I marry, you'll live with me. My home will be your home."

"I won't be any better off then than I am now. I'll still be a burden."

"I won't treat you like Mama does. You know I would never."

"I know, but, Melinda, don't you see? I've got to go. If I don't I'll just shrivel up."

"I'll shrivel without you. My sisters and Mama will stifle me as sure as I'm breathing."

"You are not the stifling kind. You'll do fine without me."

"You can't go, Becca. Your grandfather lives in Montana. Not to mention that he's a… I hate to say so, but he's a Moreland, and a stranger."

"We can't judge all Morelands by my father. In his letters, Grandfather sounds congenial. I believe he is just a sweet, little old man who wants to meet his only grandchild. No doubt at his age he's helpless and feeble. I'm sure he needs me."

"But Montana is so far away! How will you even get there?"

How indeed? She'd spent countless hours lying awake, or playing her violin, thinking it over.

"By paddleboat. It leaves here and goes right to Coulson. That's not far from my grandfather in Big Timber."

"What's not far?"

"Only about eighty miles." She shrugged and stared down at her violin case.

"Of wilderness!"

"It's not as though it's uninhabited."

"Mama will forbid it." Melinda tapped her

finger to her lips. "Paddleboats are dangerous. It will involve months of travel. Then there's the Morelands. Demons and that side of your family are one and the same to her."

"Whether they are or not, that's something I need to know for myself…before it's too late."

She stood up, pressing the violin case to her chest. Looking down at Melinda, she felt her heart thrum against it. Her need of this instrument went as deep as her need for food…deeper than her need for sleep.

The first time she had touched the gift from her grandfather, something shifted inside her. The instrument had belonged to her grandmother. According to Grandfather's letter, Catherine Moreland had a talent that could only be described as a gift.

By George, she knew this to be true even though she had never met her. There were times when she felt that her late grandmother stood behind her guiding the bow across the strings.

It was a fanciful notion, but not one that she had ever been able to rid herself of…nor did she want to. If a Moreland could possess such an exquisite gift, then just maybe they were not the reprobates that Aunt Eunice painted them to be.

"Melinda, I don't know who I am. Your mother has tried to make me into one of her own, but I just don't fit. I've got to see if it's the Moreland in me that made me kick a man in the pants."

"You know, our Grandmother Lane would have done the same. Maybe it's her you take after and not a Moreland."

"I'll never know that unless I meet my grandfather."

Melinda sighed and shook her head. "If you're set on this, you have my blessing. And don't worry about Screech. I'll take good care of him."

"I would not ask that of a saint." Screech was a green parrot with a pretty yellow-and-blue head. The bird, she had been assured, would outlive most men. Screech had been a point of stress to her aunt for as long as Rebecca had. They had been abandoned by her mother as a pair. "I'd live in constant fear that your mother might serve him up for dinner."

"That might not be the worst thing ever," Melinda declared. They laughed together. This was something that Rebecca would miss down to her bones. "We'll tell Mama first thing in the morning. You can be on your way when the next paddleboat comes through."

Melinda stood up. Arm in arm they walked slowly back to the house.

"I'm going to miss you dreadfully, cousin," Rebecca said past the lump in her throat.

Maybe it was beyond foolish to leave the only person who had ever truly loved her. But she'd gone over and over it in her head. This was something she had to do.

"Not if I go with you!" Melinda's eyes flashed up at her, sparkling blue mischief in the moonlight.

Having her cousin at her side would be wonderful. The temptation to encourage her to do so was strong…but wrong. Melinda was right about Montana being a rugged place teeming with bears, wolves and who knew what other dangers.

"You know you can't."

Melinda shrugged. "I might turn up one day, if Mama tries to give me to the butcher in your place. You'll answer your door one day and there I'll be, trailed by a wolf pack and half eaten by a bear."

Climbing the path toward the house she watched the moon dip closer to the horizon and felt the warmth of her petite cousin beside her.

She prayed that she was not making a giant mistake in leaving the familiar for the unknown.

Chapter Two

Coulson, Montana, June 1882

Lantree Walker listened to the full-bodied whistle of the *River Queen*. From where he stood on the boardwalk he watched the riverboat's twin smokestacks blow sooty smoke into the pristine sky.

A stand of trees grew between him and the dock so he couldn't see how many passengers were disembarking.

In his opinion, the fewer the better.

Not only did newcomers bring their bags and other possessions, they brought unintended disease. Fevers and plagues rarely announced their arrival.

Even Coulson, a place as wicked as they came, did not deserve to be decimated by disease.

To his bones, he felt Moreland Ranch calling

him home, where the air was fresh and the trees tickled the sky.

This was not a town a man wanted to linger in. It had more saloons than legitimate businesses and more brothels than saloons. Wild and rowdy was the rule of the day and more so, the night. This was a town without a single church to redeem the lost souls of its inhabitants.

The sooner he loaded the supplies he had purchased into the wagon and headed back home, the happier he would be.

He figured he ought to pay a visit to the barber before heading out, since his hair hung well past his shoulders. Hell, he hadn't shaved in days… since before he left the ranch.

What he ought to do was not what he was going to do. He could shave on the trail if his face itched.

A man stumbled across his path. He caught the fellow's arm to keep him from landing face-first on the boardwalk. Out of long habit he studied red eyes and felt the skin under his fingers for unnatural warmth.

As he'd suspected, the man was merely drunk, so he straightened him and pointed him on his way.

Crowds had not always made him uneasy. In

his former life, before fever had decimated Amberville, he hadn't minded them...he'd even enjoyed the hustle and bustle of town.

Not anymore. Ghosts haunted crowds.

Not the vaporous departed...but there was always the flash of a stranger's smile that reminded him of a neighbor who had died while Lantree had wiped his brow. Or the high-pitched laugh of a woman sounding like Abigail Steen, who had fought for her last breath while she gripped his hand.

He shook his head, took a long, slow breath of air. He filled his lungs with the fresh, muddy scent of the Yellowstone River.

As soon as he deposited his wages he would load the wagon and be on his way.

It was no accident that the bank was located only a few doors down from Sheriff Johnson's office. The sheriff was a giant of a man with a mean reputation. A thief, or a drunk, would think twice before robbing the bank.

He strolled past the sheriff's office with a nonchalant stride, but he was anything but relaxed.

A fresh set of wanted posters decorated the lawman's front door. He needed to look at them, but he hell and damn did not want to. The closer he got, the harder his heart beat, the more damp his armpits felt.

He slowed his pace and scanned the broadsheets. Relief eased his heart back to its normal rhythm…one more trip to town without seeing his "likeness" staring back at him.

He dreaded the day that he would see his twin brother's face staring back at him.

In spite of his brother's crime, he loved him and the thought of him being captured or killed made the blood hitch in his veins.

Then again, in an odd way, it might be a relief to see the broadsheet. It would mean he had not yet been apprehended, had not faced a noose or an itchy-fingered bounty hunter.

With that worry put to rest for the moment, he felt lighter in his soul. Home was only days away with its crisp air and polished blue sky.

The three years he had spent working for Hershal Moreland had been some of the best he had known.

Moreland Ranch was a bit of heaven on earth. Its southern border lay along the Yellowstone River and its northern border stretched to the mountains. The house had a view of both the Beartooth Range and the Crazy Mountains.

He'd spent more than a few quiet hours fish-ing Big Timber Creek where it cut through the ranch.

The land had given him a place to heal, but it was Hershal Moreland who had found a broken soul and brought him home, given him sanctuary and shown him a new way of life.

There had been a time when he'd believed that the only life he could be happy with was that of a medical doctor.

With what Boone had done, he believed he owed something to…well, he didn't know to whom, but he'd felt that dedicating his life to healing in some way made up for his brother's crime.

Life had certainly set him straight on making anything up to anybody. The fever that had swept through his town like a putrid wind claimed the old, the young, sweet mothers and their little babies.

Hadn't touched him, though. The ones who depended upon him, upon his skill as a healer, died all about him, but he remained standing with his stethoscope dangling about his stooped shoulders and his confidence buried along with most of his fiancée's family.

He'd never blamed Eloise for calling things off, not even when she'd accused him of incompetence, taken off her engagement ring and flung it out the window of the schoolhouse-turned-hospital. How could he say, with her loved ones lying dead, that she was wrong? That the bitterness in her gaze was undeserved?

Hell, he'd turned bitter against himself. He'd only really begun to live again when Hershal showed him another way. Over the past few years the old man had become more than kin.

Truly, the only person he'd been closer to in his life was Boone.

But his brother was lost to him. One thoughtless act, an accident really, had made Boone an outlaw. It had also made Lantree who he was... or had been.

"Hell, Boone," he mumbled. "Why'd you have to draw your gun?"

Rebecca had been prepared for Montana being an untamed land. During the two months she had spent aboard the *River Queen*, she'd heard stories of bears, cougars and violent storms that washed folks right away.

What she had not been prepared for was Montana's natural, shout-out-loud beauty.

Over the past week, she would barely catch

her breath over one wonder before another would appear.

She'd watched from the balustrade while the *River Queen* drifted past grassy meadows surrounded by great trees. She'd heard the wind sighing and moaning through them at night while she slept on deck, gazing up at a sky so sparkling that it seemed to be in constant, glittering movement.

It was the sight of the distant mountains, though, still capped with snow, that brought her to her knees.

Literally.

Getting off the boat a few moments ago, she had been so engrossed by their grandeur that she had tripped over a small piece of baggage that someone had carelessly left near the gangplank. She had hit her knees and stayed that way, staring at what she had been told were the Beartooth Mountains. If at that moment she had been swallowed by a bear or shredded by a cougar, Aunt Eunice would be proven right, but Rebecca would die satisfied.

Although, she realized, still on her knees and gazing at the town, the real danger might come from that direction rather than God's stunning mountain range.

Was she mistaken that even at this hour of the day the scent of alcohol wafted on the air... and tobacco? Surely her nose was oversensitive, she didn't really smell sweat and stale cologne?

Even if her nose was conjuring smells, her ears heard things quite accurately. The jarring sound of an out-of-tune piano drifted out of a saloon nearby, along with a woman's laugher, a man's cussing...and a gunshot.

By George, she had not imagined the gunshot or the one that answered it.

"Miss Lane?"

Rebecca looked up from where she knelt in the dirt to see Tom, a young, fresh-faced deckhand, looking down at her. He had her trunk slung across his shoulders.

She stood up, dusted off her skirt and tweaked her hat.

"Where would you like for me to deliver your trunk?" he asked.

Sunshine illuminated a smattering of freckles across his nose. He stared with a frown at Screech, who sat on the perch in his travel cage. The bird eyed Tom with a pivot of his yellow-and-blue head.

"Yummy," Screech said. "Here."

The bird had not made many friends on the

trip, very likely due to his tendency to nip…and screech, which he did with regularity at sunrise.

The safekeeping of her trunk was a problem. She could not have it delivered anyplace in town since she had no intention of getting closer to it than the dock.

"Where are Mrs. Henson and her daughters staying?" Perhaps she could accompany them until she figured things out. She had met the women briefly on the boat when they had come to the lower deck to check on their goods.

Tom blushed. "Those weren't her daughters, Miss Lane. They were more like…well…I reckon you'd call them recruits. They've probably taken up business at the Sullied Gully by now."

Oh, dear… They had looked like normal women. Aunt Eunice would be stricken if she discovered that the niece she had taken such pains to raise to be a lady had spoken with prostitutes. No doubt her aunt would compare them to Rebecca's mother.

Tom was beginning to show the strain of holding her trunk.

"Just leave it here beside the dock."

"But where do you aim to go?" It made her uncomfortable to see his eyes widen in alarm.

"My grandfather's ranch near Big Timber."

"That's near eighty miles, you'll need someone to get you there."

"I've been told that men who are out of work often act as guides."

"You sit tight here. Coulson's not the place for a lady like you. I'll pass the word around."

"Thank you, Tom." She handed him a quarter. "I appreciate your help."

"Don't wander off, now," he said with a doff of his cap. "I'll send someone down shortly."

She watched him saunter away. The afternoon sunshine gave him a long, fluid shadow. Tom entered the first saloon he came to.

"I hope he sends someone out soon," she said to Screech. His pupils flashed, a certain sign of his intelligence. "Because I'm not leaving our goods unattended."

To be honest, she didn't have the kind of goods that a thief might be interested in. Still, they were hers and she needed them. And there was the one item of great value, the one she didn't even dare display so close to town.

Her grandmother's violin, wrapped carefully in her spare petticoats and centered in the trunk, was more than polished wood. It was a link to the grandmother she had never known.

No matter how long it took, she would sit on

top of the trunk like a bird on her nest, keeping her precious cargo safe.

She only hoped that Tom really was arranging an escort to Moreland Ranch. A young man in a bar with alcohol, and ladies after his quarter... Well, his attention might have wandered from her plight.

"Yummy," Screech said. "Ummm, yummy."

"Yes, me, too," she answered, then settled her derriere onto the lid of the trunk.

Having finished his business at the bank, Lantree walked the isolated path that wound through the trees behind the main street of town.

The boardwalk in front of the establishments would have been a quicker way to get back to his wagon, but this way was more peaceful, more private.

Unfortunately, this path tended to be a dumping ground for drunks who had been tossed from the saloons. He spotted one now, face down in a mud puddle.

With the inebriated as plentiful as fleas on a hound, no one much cared if one of them never came out of his stupor. Boot Hill was home to a fair share of unfortunate alcoholics.

Lantree crouched down beside the man. His

skin was an unhealthy color. He touched the man's throat, feeling for a pulse.

It was there, sluggish under his fingertips. Turning the fellow over, he sighed. The drunk was more a boy than a man. If he kept up this behavior he wouldn't live long enough to grow a full beard.

"Let's get you out of here," he said. Slinging the limp body over his shoulder, he stood up.

The closest thing to a doctor that Coulson could boast was the bartender at the Gilded Cage Saloon. "Doc" Brody had assisted an army doctor for three years so he did what he was able.

Brody would have enough skill to see the kid back to sobriety.

Lantree walked past the *River Queen* on his way to the Gilded Cage. Only one passenger remained in sight.

This one straggler made him pivot at the hip, stop and stare. She sat upon a trunk beside the dock, apparently conversing with a large green bird in a dome-shaped cage.

Decent women in Coulson were rare. Perhaps she was a lady of the night, but if that were the case, she would just be starting her career.

Her skin looked fresh…lovely even. Her expression was bright and untroubled.

Evidently, the bird must have done something funny because the woman laughed out loud. She didn't try to hide her amusement coyly behind her hand, but let it out, lifting her face to the sky, looking joyful.

He wanted to weep for her. Give the girl six months, and she would be visiting Doc Brody with sores that she would never recover from.

Maybe he ought to sit down beside her and warn her of the danger, but he had the boy slung over his shoulder.

At any rate, the young woman would resent his interference and he was in no position to advise or heal anyone.

Still, it was a shame to imagine such beauty fading to despair and illness.

A few moments later, he deposited the boy on a chair inside the Gilded Cage.

He approached the bar and signaled Brody with a wave.

"That one's no more than a kid," he explained to the "Doctor" and pushed a five-dollar bill in his direction. "See what you can do to get him sober."

"You and your strays, Lantree." The bartender poured him a shot of amber-colored whiskey. "Just a dram to keep you warm on the ride home."

"Appreciate it, Doc."

He took a sip, enjoying the smooth heat sliding down his throat, warming his belly.

At the other end of the bar, a young man...a deckhand from the *Queen*, he thought, chatted with Big Nosed Mike. No one knew Mike's real name, but everyone knew about his bullish reputation...everyone apparently but the boy chatting amiably with him.

Lantree slugged down the rest of his drink. Coulson was wearing on his nerves. The sooner he got home to the tranquility of the ranch, the happier he would be.

On his way out the door, he paused to straighten the boy in his chair and check his pulse one more time.

He'd recover this time, but if no one took him in hand he faced a sad, short future.

Outside, June sunshine warmed his face, but come tonight the weather would turn downright cold. It was a lucky thing he'd purchased several heavy blankets and a couple of rain slickers.

"Walker!" came a voice from behind him on the boardwalk. "Hold up a minute."

He'd hoped to get in and out of town without

a confrontation with William Smothers, Coulson's power-hungry mayor.

He stopped, turned. When he did, he spotted the fresh young woman with the bird. She was standing beside her trunk, stretching. She was tall, very tall, with a lithe, lovely figure. He wished…well, he wished for a lot of things, but it was a shame about the girl.

Smothers gazed up at him, yanking then smoothing the lapels of his fancy suit over his portly belly. "I heard you were in town."

"Just on my way out."

"Arrange a meeting for me with your boss." As usual, Smothers was short and to the point.

The fellow was shifty, all right. Just because he wore a tailored suit and polished boots didn't make him any less of a snake.

"Mr. Moreland sends his regards and his regrets."

"See here, Lantree. The railroad is coming. This town is going to grow up overnight. We need lumber. Moreland's got more trees than he needs."

"Not interested."

Smothers might yak all day without Hershal giving up so much as a branch.

He'd refused to sell it to fuel the steamboats.

He'd escorted the railroad folks off his land with a shotgun. His boss was as protective of his trees as he might have been with his own kin, if he'd had any.

There was the granddaughter, but her mother's family had poisoned her opinion of Moreland. The girl would never come here, no matter how much comfort she would be able to give the old man.

"You arrange a meeting, and I'll make it worth your while. How much do you make as ramrod for Moreland? Not as much as you'd like, I'd be willing to bet."

"I watch out for Moreland's interests."

"Just deliver the message this time." Smothers's face began to mottle. A red circle blotched his nose. "Or I'll find another, not-so-gentle way of delivering it."

"Is that a threat, Smothers?" Lantree took a step closer, bent down to the mayor's level and spoke softly. "I reckon you didn't mean it to be."

"I want those trees."

"Get them somewhere else."

"You know that property has the best lumber, and all near the river. We need it and we need it fast if Coulson is going to be the railhead and not Billings. The survival of this town depends on it."

One more reason for Hershal to hold on to his trees, as far as Lantree was concerned. If the railroad boss picked another place for his town and this one died, so much the better.

"If you try anything illegal, I'll know it, Smothers."

He walked away, leaving the man steaming in his fancy duds.

Home, Moreland Ranch, could not come soon enough.

Thanks to Tom, Rebecca had a guide. She watched while the squat but solid-looking man built a campfire for the night.

To appearances, Mike looked like a ruffian, with shaggy hair that could use a wash, along with the rest of him. But this was a rugged land, full of rugged men, and she would not judge his character by his grooming habits. Besides, Tom would not have sent him to her unless he was of dependable character.

Wisely, she had only paid him half his due, the rest to be delivered upon her safe arrival at Moreland Ranch. Even if Mike did not care about her welfare in a personal sense, he would want the rest of his money.

If nothing else, her guide did build a roaring fire. The flames chased away some of the chill setting in, now that the sun had set. She walked to her trunk where it was stored for the night beside the pair of saddles lying on the ground.

If the rest of the journey went as easily as the first three hours, it would be a pleasant trip.

She withdrew a key from the pocket of her skirt, opened the trunk, then lifted out her coat and shrugged it on.

Mike glanced over at her with a grin.

Compared to the place she had grown up, Montana was big and wild. In Kansas City, one ran into folks on every street corner. Here in the wild, even street corners were scarce.

She listened to the night sounds, how they all blended, composing a song. When she closed her eyes, she could clearly pick out the melody created by a pair of hooting owls. The sough of the breeze through the treetops made up the chorus. Far away, lifting on the wind, she heard what sounded like a man's voice, but was more likely the yipping and yapping of a pack of coyotes on a distant hilltop.

"Beans?" Kneeling by the fire, Mike pivoted

on his knee, his face lit up like a gap-toothed jack-o'-lantern. He lifted a can in his fist. "Ain't much of a cook, so to speak, but I can warm beans."

"Thank you, Mike." She smiled brightly at him. Since they would be journeying together for a couple of days, they might as well be cordial. "Anything warm would be a dream come true."

He stared at her for an uncomfortable moment, nodded his head, then shot her a sidelong wink.

How odd.

Ten minutes later, they sat beside the fire, each with a mug of warm beans cupped in their palms.

"How long do you reckon that birdie of yours is going to last?" Mike pointed his fork at Screech, who sat on his perch grooming his pretty feathers beside the fire.

"What do you mean?"

"It's a tough land, ma'am. Most critters tend to blend in. That one's bright as a fancy gewgaw." Mike picked a fragment of bean from his teeth with his fork tine and flicked it into the fire. "For an extra dollar, I could make sure he doesn't get mistaken for a chicken."

A chicken? Was the man daft? Show her the

chicken that spoke English and had feathers so pretty they were iridescent in the sunshine.

She would like nothing more than to set her guide straight but she held her tongue, wanting to keep things friendly between them.

"Since it's only the two of us, I can't think that will happen."

"Someone not as civilized as you and me might come along. Have themselves a right fancy dinner."

A chill skittered up her spine wondering if he was truly concerned about Screech, or if that had been a veiled threat. How was she to know?

She was suddenly uncomfortable being alone in the forest with a strange man whose only recommendation was that he was available when no one else was, and he claimed to know the way to Moreland Ranch.

By George, she had better sleep with Screech's cage on her lap. A woman in her situation could not be too careful.

"We seem so isolated out here," she pointed out. "Is there really much danger of someone coming upon us?"

He slid toward her two inches. She slid six the other way.

"There's wild things out there in the dark…

bears, wolves, wildcats…wilder men. But don't you worry, pretty lady. Big Mike is here to see to your needs."

That ought to be a comfort, but the hair rose on the back of her neck and the goose bumps on her arms.

Tom, she had to remind herself, would not have sent her off with an unsavory fellow.

"Any beast or ruffian shows up, you run to me, snuggle in good and tight." He opened his arms. She scooted away. "Come on, girlie, give it a practice."

"If the time comes, I'll know what to do." She eyed the iron kettle sitting on a rock beside the fire.

"I don't know about you, but I plan to keep good and warm tonight," he mumbled.

His gaze wandered over her, slow and overly familiar. He scooted his rump uncomfortably close.

Suddenly his gaze jerked up, spotting something over her shoulder.

Her "protector's" expression hardened. His lips peeled back in a snarl.

"Move away from the woman," came a deep voice from behind her.

Oh, goodness. They were not as isolated as

she had assumed. An intruder had come upon them without crunching a leaf.

She turned to see one of the ruffians Mike had warned of…a very large ruffian.

He had to be more than six and a half feet tall! In a moment, when she stood to defend herself she would have to look up at him.

Firelight reflected off his solid-looking form. The evening breeze blew streams of long blond hair in front of his face. Golden highlights flickered in the strands. It distracted her that his hair gleamed with cleanliness.

What kind of ruffian had clean hair and the build of a handsome Viking?

It didn't matter what kind. A ruffian was a ruffian…and he was threatening her guide.

Her guide who, faced with danger, did not open his arms to protect her as he'd promised.

"Go find your own way to get warm tonight." Mike stood, growled and balled his fists, clearly ready to protect his own pitiful self.

The intruder, rather than backing off, took several steps toward Mike.

Mike scuttled backward, nearly tripping over a large rock.

Screech began to screech when Mike began to holler about the man having no claim on her.

And, by the dickens, no man did!

Since the men were railing at each other and paying no attention to her, it was an easy matter to seize the iron bean kettle and swing it at the giant's head from behind.

He crumpled to his knees, grasping his temples in his large fists.

Mike did not take that moment to defend her. Instead of tying up the disabled villain, he dashed for her trunk. He lifted the unlocked lid. Somehow, he seemed to know exactly where she kept her money. He plucked it out.

She ran after him, swinging the kettle, but he was up on his horse before she could do more than land a blow to his calf.

In his rush to get away, he left the older horse, the one she had been riding, and both saddles.

In all fairness, the animal and the abandoned belongings now belonged to her.

She would name the horse Hoodwinked.

"Screech! Be quiet!"

The bird obeyed for a full two seconds before declaring, "Uh-oh."

This was a fine mess! Abandoned in the forest with a wounded criminal. Lost with no idea how to get to Moreland Ranch.

At least this fellow couldn't steal her money.

And, the kettle gripped tightly in her fist, she would fight for her virtue.

Let the man make a move, let him utter one untoward thing, and she'd smash his nose. She would batter his ears and knock out his teeth.

He looked up at her, silent. The light of the campfire revealed the intense blue of his eyes.

What kind of brigand had eyes like that? And perfect white teeth…and clean hair?

Surely his voice would give him away as an evildoer. Curse words would probably accent his every utterance.

"You're a fair hand with a kettle, ma'am."

"And I'm not afraid to use it again."

He touched the back of his head. His long fingers came away streaked with blood. He swayed on his knees.

She hurried to Mike's abandoned saddle packs, looking for some sort of binding and found a short section of rope.

"Are you twins?" the man asked. "Or just one lady?"

"Triplets… Give me your wrists and don't try anything."

"I'll try not to be sick."

His hands hung limp at his sides so she

snatched them up and made quick work of tethering them.

All at once he lurched forward. His weight knocked her to the ground.

By the saints, this was a muddle. Not only was she lost in the wilderness, but she now had a questionable man's bleeding head cradled on her bosom.

She wriggled and pushed until the man's head lay in her lap. Humph! He had long eyelashes, sandy and dark at the same time…and lovely hair that she wanted to… Well, quite honestly, she wanted to stroke it.

Perhaps she should have paid attention to Aunt Eunice, who had announced that she would come to ruin in Montana.

Still, she wasn't ruined, at least not as long as her captive remained passed out.

A strand of hair streaked with blood lay across his cheek. She brushed it aside with her thumb and felt the rough scrape of his beard under her skin.

She had never been this close to a full-bodied man before, had never smelled the scent of warm masculine breath so close to her face. She certainly had never pressed her hand on one's chest, feeling muscles and ribs rise and fall.

This, and she could only be honest, was a handsome man.

And as long as she was being honest, what was there to indicate that he had been up to no good?

Her assumption, was all. Thinking back on it, Mike was the one who had been taking liberties.

This man had simply demanded that Mike back away.

Oh, dear, had she beaned her defender? All of a sudden she felt horrible. If his intention had been to protect, she owed him a great deal.

Then again, if he had only wanted to take Mike's place, she still owed him a great deal.

From a distance not far off, a wolf howled. She glanced at the smear of blood on the man's cheek, hoping that the scent would not attract predators.

The safety and the warmth that the fire provided would not last all night.

"Wake up, mister."

She gently patted his cheek but he did not stir.

No matter who he was, she wanted him awake.

By the look of him, and the solid weight of bone and muscle lying across her, he was a fellow who would be able to fend off a wolf without trouble…maybe even a bear.

"I'm sorry I hit you. Please wake up."

His eyeballs moved under the lids, but other than that he did not stir.

After a while, the fire grew dimmer. The warmth receded and a bitter chill rushed to fill its place. It would haunt her conscience forever if she allowed her captive to freeze to death.

She shrugged her arms out of her coat, draped it over her shoulders, then spread the long tails over her hero or assailant.

It only covered him to his knees, but some warmth was beginning to build between their bodies.

A very curious warmth. It seemed to come from within her.

If she survived until morning, she would think more about it. Just now, the events of the day had worn her through.

She huddled over the man and tried to relax, but she was more than half-certain that eyes peered at her from the brush.

Chapter Three

Lantree scented a woman.

He cracked open his eyes but saw things through a dark blur. Yep, his surroundings had been doused in oil. Objects swayed like pond grass underwater.

Apparently his mind was still feeling the effects of the blow to his head, which was to be expected. In all likelihood the woman whose face swam in his smoky vision was not real.

That didn't keep him from finding her interesting.

She was asleep with her face nodding over him. It seemed that his head was lying in her lap and they were both huddling under some sort of covering.

No one had ever reported that hallucinations came with smells, but he breathed in the sweet scent of femininity.

He didn't mind that, not one bit. Neither did he mind that the vision had the face of an angel. Long dark lashes rested on high cheekbones. Her eyes moved under her eyelids as though she were dreaming. Pretty lips lay still in slumber. If the hallucination awoke and smiled what would her mouth look like?

Even more, what would it taste like if he could lift his head high enough to give those slumbering lips a kiss?

He wouldn't try though, because he knew that doing so would make the vision disappear into a puff of forgotten dream.

As much as he wanted to indulge in this fantasy, his head hurt like hell and his stomach churned. He needed to close his eyes.

What a shame though, to wake tomorrow and not recall her.

Regretfully, he closed his eyes and gave himself over to oblivion.

The lilting melody of "The Morning Suite" from *Peer Gynt* woke him. It was beautiful, but distressing. Heavenly music could only indicate that he had died from the blow to his head.

Odd, he hadn't felt it to be a life-or-death wound.

He opened his eyes to see the first rays of daylight touching the treetops. He listened, afraid to move or breathe…but he was breathing.

While dead men might listen to divine music upon fluffy clouds, they did not breathe.

Mortal pain shot through his head. His pulse throbbed and he ached all over. He was most certainly alive.

But there was music.

He sat up, stifling a groan.

He glanced about, looking for the source of the melody.

It had been an age since he had heard a symphonic piece, another lifetime. Only now did he realize how much he'd missed it. Before the epidemic, Lantree had been a frequent visitor to the theater. There had been few things he enjoyed more than sitting quietly and listening to classical melodies.

He turned his head, and a stabbing pain made him wish he hadn't…until he saw the figure standing on the rise of the hill, half-hidden among the trees.

A woman bathed in morning light drew her bow over the strings of a violin.

She swayed while she played, her trim figure seeming to be one with the music. While he watched she closed her eyes and turned in a circle, her skirt twirling gently about her long legs.

Sunshine glittered on her lips.

So that was what they looked like when they smiled. The memory of her came back to him now. She was the angel from his dream.

He glanced at the sunlight creeping down the trees. From their branches, birds began to sing along with the violin.

In this instant, life was beautiful…ugliness did not exist.

Losing himself in the moment, he was certain that the melody came from the woman rather than the instrument.

Then a bird screeched. Not a pretty morning coo or a gentle twitter, but a grating on the ears that had to be disturbing the peace for miles around.

The woman lowered her instrument. She pivoted with a scowl.

"Be quiet, Screech! You don't need to copy every—" Her eyes widened when she saw him. "Oh! Good morning… By George, you don't look half-bad considering…well, that you were hit by a kettle."

Beauty incarnate gazed, wide-eyed, at him… so did the young prostitute from the dock.

She hurried down the rise in long strides. She stopped at a large travel trunk and put her violin inside then closed the lid.

He stood up because she was walking toward him now and he wanted to judge how tall she really was.

He was used to women much shorter. The top of her head would neatly tuck under his chin were he holding her in an embrace.

The temptation to get aquatinted in a carnal way was hard to ignore. With her size, he would not have to worry about hurting her during—

He wouldn't know her that way, of course. He'd taken the Hippocratic oath. It went bone deep in spite of how things had turned out. That bit about doing no harm meant something to him. To consort with such a woman, especially one so new to the trade, would most certainly do her harm.

"Well, to be truthful…" She stood four feet away and she smelled the same as she had last night…sweet and female to the core. "I'm the one who hit you with the kettle."

He nodded and glanced about the campsite, wondering what had become of his team and wagon.

"I do beg your pardon." She wrung her hands

in front of her. "I thought you were a thief…or worse."

"Reckon that's understandable since I did sneak up on you in the dark."

"Sit down here, mister. Your skin still looks like milk."

She pointed to a spot beside the long-cold embers of the campfire.

He did feel peaked so he eased down onto the spot.

"Can you eat something?" she asked then hurried toward a pair of saddlebags. She rifled through them, frowning.

"I figure Mike owes me a meal… Oh, here's some jerked beef, at least."

The soiled dove knelt before him, looking fresh as morning. Women of her kind tended to look drawn and haggard at this time of day due to being active all night.

"Can you eat some, do you think?" She held the dried beef toward him. "I'd feel ever so much better if you did."

In spite of how his stomach still felt queasy, he took a bite. It wasn't half as bad as he feared so he took another.

The relief in her expression made him take a third bite and nod his thanks while he chewed.

With a smile, she sat across from him, her legs tucked beneath her. He couldn't help but wonder what legs like that would look like in all their bare, long-limbed glory.

For a dollar, he'd be able to find out. If he were another kind of man—one like Mike, say—he would.

Instead, he sighed and wondered.

"It's not my business and you can say so, but why did you come out here with Mike, that is, why did you leave the safety of town?"

"First of all, I doubt that Coulson is all that safe. But Mike and I had business together. Business which he reneged on."

"If you don't mind my saying so, that was for the best."

"I can't imagine why you would think so." She reached across the cold fire pit. "Here, turn your head so I can see that lump."

"It's not the worst I've ever had. I'll do."

The young whore broke a piece of the jerky off then leaned sideways to give it to the bird.

"Yummy," the green-feathered creature said three times while holding the beef in one claw and happily nibbling on it.

"I've got to go see to my team and wagon. But wait here, I'll be back," he said.

"I've already taken care of them. I heard your horses neighing after…after things settled down last night. I brought them here. See, there they are down by the stream."

"You wandered away from the safety of the fire?"

"There wasn't much help for it unless I wanted to leave your poor beasts unattended."

"There are wild things out there, miss. You're lucky you didn't meet up with any of them."

"I'd prefer a wild beast to a wild man. When was the last time you heard of a bear stealing a woman's savings? The same cannot be said of Mike."

"He is a bad one." A lecture might be out of line but hell if he could keep himself from giving it. "I'm sorry about your money, miss. Have you spent a long time earning it?"

"I began when I was fourteen." She sighed, clearly disgusted. "To think of the hours I gave to the single gentlemen of Kansas City. I wore myself out, up all hours, often by candlelight, and all so that miserable creature, Mike, could ride off with what I had earned."

"There's more than money you might have lost…your health for one thing."

"I feel fit as a fiddle, thank you very much."

"That's because you are young…and you've been lucky with the men you have serviced."

"Might I point out that they were the lucky ones? I gave them fair exchange for every dollar. Even though I was young I put my heart into what I did."

"As admirable as that is…you are going to end up sick. Your way of life will kill you."

"And what do you know about my way of life? We are all but strangers."

"I saw you yesterday, at the dock sitting on your trunk."

"Which led you to believe that sitting in God's glorious country on a trunk lid will lead to illness?"

"Let me show you where it leads."

Taking her to the Sullied Gully and showing her what her future would be might save her life.

He reached for her hand.

She reached for the kettle.

The hand reaching for her was nicely formed, the fingers long and rugged.

That did not in any way mean that she was going to allow them to touch her.

Hadn't she learned at her aunt's knee and by

her mother's example, that virtue, once given away, could not be regained?

"You," she said with her fingers solidly gripping the handle of the kettle, "will not show me a single thing unless you want a matching lump on the other side of your skull."

"What if I pay you? I'll give you a dollar, just like any other man, for half a day of your time."

It would take far less time than that for her to mend his shirt. But that would mean him removing it and his attitude was far too familiar as it was. Besides, her needles and thread were at the bottom of her trunk and she did not want to turn her back on him for the time it would take to fish them out.

It was becoming clear that the men of the mountains were a greater danger than the wildlife. Tom had shown a severe lack of judgment. Mike was a thief. And this man whose name she didn't even know wanted to show her what there was about her life that was going to lead to ruin and death.

He might be delusional from the blow…or he might be insane.

She would be much better off on her own.

"Kindly take your beasts and your goods and leave my campsite."

"Two dollars then."

She stared him down hard.

"Three dollars and not a penny more," he added.

Now he was beginning to tempt her. Three dollars to repair a rip in his shirt…one that was too small to even be seen? And she with not a cent to her name?

"Four dollars and we have a bargain."

"I'm being robbed."

"Be that as it may, if you want my services, you will set four dollars beside Screech's cage and take off your shirt."

"I'll keep it on if it's all the same to you," he said then dug into his pocket and withdrew four one-dollar bills. He set them beside Screech, who eyed them with flashing eyes.

"How do you expect me to do my job with you still in your clothing?"

"All I want is your time…to help you understand the life a young lady like you can expect to lead if you continue on the way you are."

"You don't make much sense. I'm sorry. Your confusion is my fault and I do apologize. Won't you see a doctor about your head? Here, take back one dollar. It's only fair since I'm the one who injured you."

She stood up, brushed a leaf from her skirt and went to fetch the needle and thread. It wouldn't be easy to find among the many skirts, blouses, petticoats and stockings that Melinda had insisted she bring.

At length, she found a needle and selected a color of thread that, surprisingly, matched his shirt. She threaded the needle while she walked back to her client.

This was not going to be an easy job with him still in the shirt. She only prayed that the rip was not in an inconvenient spot.

"I may have to touch you," she warned him. "Just keep in mind that this is strictly business. Once I'm finished you will go on your way and I'll go on mine."

He gazed at the needle and thread looking perplexed. Had he never had a garment repaired for pity's sake?

She sat down beside him, running her fingers over the arm seams of his shirt. Not even a loose thread to be worried about.

Clearing her throat she began to yank the shirt from the waistband of his pants. Truly, this could not be more uncomfortable.

"You misunderstand," he said, his breath

seeming to come short and fast. "I only want to talk to you."

The only decent thing to do was humor the man. Perhaps by talking, he might become more sensible.

She pinned the threaded needle through her collar so as not to lose it.

"Do you often pay for conversation, Mister...?"

"Walker," he said. "And no, I've never paid for it."

"It's the blow to your head making you do so, no doubt." She folded her hands in her lap, ready to do her duty and listen to whatever nonsense he had to spout. "Please, feel free to have your say."

"Ladies of the night," he began then cleared his throat. "They lead a hard life...a short life."

"No doubt that's true."

"They meet up with brutal men. If a woman is lucky enough to survive the harsh treatment, she rarely survives the syphilis, gonorrhea and other sexually transmitted diseases."

Now he had her blushing. How could she not when he spoke so boldly of inappropriate matters?

She half wished she had not accepted his

money…and certainly that she had not walloped him in the head.

"I'm sure that's very sad," she agreed, hoping that this conversation would turn to a more respectable subject.

"You don't seem overly worried, but I can assure you the danger is very real."

"Maybe you'd like to talk about something more pleasant," she urged.

"I'd like to convince you to earn a living in some other way."

"Mr. Walker, I've never heard of anyone becoming ill over a needle prick… Well, there was Snow White's mother, she died, but that was a fairy tale."

"You make light of the problem, but it's very real."

She sighed. How could she not? "Sometimes a body just needs a dash of humor. Don't you agree?"

"I do not. In fact, I've got a mind to tie you to a horse, haul you back to town and show you how funny a sick whore is."

She slid the needle from her collar and pointed it at him.

"I know how to use this. Lay a hand on me and I'll stitch your fingers together."

"Damned Hippocratic oath," he mumbled.

He stood up. From where she sat gazing up, it looked like his head skimmed the treetops.

"What an odd thing to say," she mumbled back.

Insanity was his problem, she decided, not the blow to his head. In some way this was a relief. His behavior was not her fault.

But then again, she was alone in the wilderness with a lunatic.

In a move too swift for her to avoid, he reached down and snatched her arm. He tossed her over his shoulder and began to walk away... somewhere.

Her horse was not saddled. His team was grazing. Did he mean to walk back to Coulson carrying her like a bag of potatoes?

Given his mental state, perhaps he did.

But given her determination not to go anywhere with him... Well, they would see who went where.

She kicked her legs but all she managed to do was cover his face in a blizzard of furious petticoats.

She screamed, having forgotten in the moment that her bird loved nothing more than to join in a ruckus.

Screech screeched. Other birds copied him and soon the branches were alive with alarmed twitters.

"I'm warning you to put me down!"

"This is for your own good," her captor grumbled.

Apparently, he had forgotten that she still gripped the needle in her hand.

Something stung him in the rump. It was early in the day for hornets.

He swatted his backside then got stung on the hand.

He spun about, gripping the woman by the knees, while he sought to slap the bug.

Sunshine glinted off something in the soiled dove's hand. All of a sudden he remembered the needle.

That's what he got for trying to do a good deed. The same sort of thing had happened to him once when he tried to set the leg of an injured raccoon. He'd been bitten. Infection had been the pay for his effort.

"What the hell, ma'am!" He didn't believe in cursing before women, but she sliced the needle at him again as he was setting her to her feet. "Damnation!"

"Escaped from bedlam or not, you have no right to accost ladies in the forest!" She backed away from him jabbing the slender weapon at the air.

He did not follow. He rubbed his wounds. Bedlam?

"I warned you what I would do. You should have known that a seamstress would know how to wield a needle."

All of a sudden he felt heat suffuse his face.

"You're not a whore?" What a colossal blunder he had made.

The woman paled.

"I beg your pardon?" she gasped and clutched one hand to her throat.

"No, I beg yours."

"What could possibly have led you to believe that I was…of that profession?"

Her cheeks were now flushing with anger, he reckoned, and rightly so.

He was an ass…a moron. No wonder she thought he belonged in bedlam.

"You were a woman alone in Coulson, for one." He had to at least try and explain his mistake.

"I didn't know that was an offense."

"I offered you money and you took it."

"And why not. I don't mend shirts for free… and by the saints, I'd like my dollar back since your addled state of mind is not my fault after all."

"So when you wanted to take off my shirt, it was to mend it?"

It's a damn good thing he hadn't acted on the urgings of his body and stripped off his shirt and everything else.

"Why else would I have asked—? Oh, my glory… You thought— I can't even say it out loud. I only meant to mend your rip."

Her face was as red as his felt.

"So—" once more, she pinned the needle to her collar "—you are not a lunatic?"

"And you are not—?" Clearly, she was not. He was an idiot to have assumed so in the first place. "In danger of catching some fatal disease?"

"Not in that way, by the saints."

With nothing left to say that did not make him sound a bigger fool than he was, he stood looking down, but not too far down, at her, silent as a stone.

He had to look like a big lump of stupid. No whore that he had ever treated, regardless of her age, had ever looked luminous. He should have seen the truth from the beginning.

All at once the seamstress's lips twitched at the corners. She covered her mouth with the back of her hand, then let it drop while she let out a full, joyous-sounding laugh.

He braced his hands on his knees, bent at the waist and laughed along with her. It felt good to laugh so freely. He couldn't recall the last time he had done that.

"So," he said when he caught his breath, "I well and truly apologize for assuming the worst of you. Please forgive me."

"It only makes us even when you think about it." She dabbed a tear from the corner of one eye. "I assumed that you were a ruffian out to do me and Mike harm. I truly apologize to you, as well."

He extended his hand and she took it. The shake of truce was slower and more intimate than it might have been, because her hand met his, dainty, sweet...and not swallowed whole.

That was something... So different from how Eloise's hand had ever felt. Eloise had been delicate, like a pretty porcelain cup that he had to be careful not to chip. Even if his fiancée hadn't walked out, she would never have fit in the life he lived now.

For all that this woman was tall and, he

thought, fit of frame, a woman was a woman and this land was hard.

Unbidden, thoughts of courting her flitted across his mind. He dashed them out quick.

Hell, he might fantasize until Kingdom Come and it wouldn't matter. A wife was someone who would need protecting and that was one big responsibility that he didn't want.

But there it came again, a vision of her and him, as irritating as a fly buzzing about the head. Mentally, he swatted at it, but it stuck to him. What might he do if things were different? He couldn't help but imagine.

He would spend some time getting to know this lady, work up to giving her a kiss.

He shook his head. Things were what they were.

"I can't help but wonder, knowing what I do now, what you were doing out here with Mike."

"Oh, that." Her expression sobered. "I hired him to take me to my grandfather's ranch. I'm in a bit of a morass now, I suppose."

"Who is your grandfather?" Maybe he knew the man and could be of help.

"Hershal Moreland, of Moreland Ranch." She sighed and shrugged her shoulders. "Maybe you know a guide who would be willing to take me there for four…oh, all right, three dollars."

Well, hell if it hadn't felt like the earth had swallowed him whole.

Here was the mysterious, and in his mind self-ish, granddaughter, come at last. He had long doubted that she would. What was she after, was what he wanted to know.

The old man's land, maybe. Or had the mayor of Coulson somehow discovered her existence and convinced her to come and persuade Moreland to sell his trees? Was the money that Mike took perhaps payment from Smothers?

If so, she would be one sorry young woman. As long as Lantree had a breath in him, she would not cheat her grandfather out of his ranch or sell the trees that Catherine Moreland had so loved.

Hell and double damn. Why couldn't Miss Moreland have simply been a whore?

Chapter Four

While it was true that Mr. Lantree was not a lunatic, it was equally true that he was sullen, stone-faced and, in spite of his handsome appearance, not enjoyable company.

While Rebecca could only be grateful for the good fortune that had landed her with Grandfather's foreman and that he happened to be on the way to Moreland Ranch, it was regrettable that she was spending endless hours sitting on the wagon bench beside a great Viking of a fellow who seemed dedicated to pointing out this and that danger.

Why, to hear him go on, one would think he didn't appreciate the majestic beauty all around. The Good Lord's creative hand was everywhere, from the great snowcapped mountains to the delicate blue flower that Mr. Walker had just rolled the wagon over and crushed.

"Do you mind if we make a short stop?" she asked when he paused in his description of how boulders rolled down from hillsides without warning and if one were lucky enough to get out of the way one must still be quick-footed enough to escape the nest of poisonous snakes that the dislodged rock had exposed.

"I mind," he snapped. "It will be a good long time before we find a suitable place to rest."

She suspected he was lying because just to the right was a lovely green meadow with a clear pool created by a waterfall tumbling down the mountainside.

"I believe, Mr. Walker, that you are trying to scare me away. I can't imagine why, but I do believe it."

"Why would I want to prevent the tender reunion between you and your grandfather?" He glanced at her from under a frown.

"I can't imagine." She squirmed on the wood bench. She really did need a moment of privacy. "Not that it is any of your concern, but it will not be a reunion. I've never met my grandfather before."

"What makes you want to meet him now?"

"Also none of your business." She would have gladly carried on a pleasant conversation, telling him about how she had never fit in at home and did not wish to marry the butcher. And most of all, that she hoped to find the family link she had been missing.

She would have liked to pass the time becoming acquainted, but ever since he'd discovered who she was he'd been as sour as curdled milk.

"Anything to do with Moreland is my business."

That was a telling statement. Either he was devoted to her grandfather or he dominated him.

"Are you related to Grandfather? Are we perhaps distant cousins?"

"We are not."

That was a relief. She had no wish to be related to such a scowler.

"I really do need to stop for a few moments."

"Later."

"If you aim this wagon at one more bump in the path, Mr. Fount of Joy, things will get messy."

It was a forward thing to say but she was desperate.

He hauled the team up short, leaped off, then stomped to her side of the wagon to help her down.

His hand under her elbow was firm, its

strength and support not unpleasant as he helped her down. She wasn't used to being in the presence of a man who was bigger than she was. The humbling fact was that she had never allowed a man to help her down from anything for fear that she would topple him.

As soon as her boot touched the ground he let go of her.

"Watch out for falling rocks," he advised.

What a shame that such a handsome face was wasted on scowls.

"While I'm at it, I'll be sure to sidestep snakes."

Seeking a private spot, she lifted the hem of her skirt and hurried across the small green meadow. What a shame to step on the tiny flowers dotting the ground, but there were so many of them it was difficult not to.

There was a large, dense bush growing beside the water so she stepped behind it. Glancing up the side of the mountain she listened to the rush of the waterfall. If only it were possible to capture the melody with her violin.

Had her grandmother ever managed it? It broke her heart that she had not been able to meet her father's mother. Sadly, the first time she had ever heard from her grandfather, was when he sent the violin after Grandmother's passing. That had been three years ago.

Sometimes she could not help but wonder what her life would have been like if her mother had been respectable and her father not a rolling stone. Perhaps she would have grown up the apple…or at least the pineapple…of her grandparents' eye.

The love of a parent was something she had missed as a child…and still did. It was her daily prayer that she would find something of that with her grandfather.

He'd given her Grandmother's violin, an item that must be precious to him. Surely that indicated that he wanted a loving relationship, too.

Still, Aunt Eunice had warned that she was going to live with the devil and that he could not possibly be anything else, given that he had produced Rebecca's father. But by that reasoning, it might be said that her grandfather could believe that Rebecca was a young woman of loose morals since that was what her mother had been.

That was certainly the first impression she had made on the grumpy Viking, and all because she had been sitting on a trunk lid.

Well, by George, she was here to find out

what was truth and what was fear. For better or worse she was going to get to know her grandfather.

And why not? She had nothing to lose but everything to gain.

With her bladder finally relieved, she straightened her clothing and stepped out from behind the bush.

She had to take two quick steps backward to avoid trampling on a kitten. The water in the pond dampened her boots.

Oh, my, but it was a sweet-looking thing with its blue eyes and fuzzy, buff-colored fur.

Looking up, it meowed and swiped at her skirt.

"My goodness, you brave little thing."

She squatted and reached her hand toward it. A rough, pink tongue licked her palm.

"Where's your mama, little one?" She waggled her fingers. "You haven't gotten lost…or become an orphan, I hope."

That was entirely possible if this land was as untamed as folks said.

"Poor little lamb."

The kitten nudged her finger with its pink nose. By the saints, one could hardly let the dear creature perish. Although if she took it with her, she couldn't imagine what she would do with it when it was fully grown.

In spite of the fact that it looked as cuddly as a house cat, it was a pint-size cougar. Perhaps if it were raised with love from infancy, it would grow up tame.

On the other hand, it might turn one day and eat her.

All she did know was that here in the moment, there was a lost baby in need of mothering, and since she would never be a mother to a human, perhaps fate had given her a cub to care for.

Or maybe she was a fool and the cub's mother was hidden in the trees ready to tear her to—

A shotgun blast rocked the tranquil meadow. Bits of tree bark fell on her hair. The kitten scurried into the brush.

Startled, she fell backward, rump-first, into the water.

The pool could only be a degree short of icing over. She shot to her feet, shivering and breathing in the scent of gunpowder.

Mr. Walker strode forward, his long, angry-looking strides convincing her that he had indeed come from Vikings…and history notwithstanding, not so long ago.

He snagged her about the waist and dragged her roughly across the meadow.

She had never been handled roughly by a man. The fact was, for good or ill, she had never been handled by a man at all.

It was odd. For all the power those large hands exerted dragging her toward the wagon, his touch caused her no pain. She would not be bruised.

For a spinster to feel the arms of a hulking male clamped about her middle…by glory, it was a thing to remember.

What a shame he was cursing in her ear.

He tossed her onto the wagon bed as though she weighed no more than Melinda did. She landed on a large bag of coffee beans, belly-first.

Why, the colossal nerve! Why, the—

Why did she suddenly feel so warm?

Anger, naturally, she deduced when her heart quit galloping like a horse outrunning a prairie fire.

In no way was it because she seemed caught in his intense blue gaze, unable to look away even though she ought to.

"Did you want me to have to explain to the old man that I let his tenderfoot granddaughter get mauled by a mountain lion?"

She scrambled to her knees. Frowning down at him, she swiped at her soaking bodice.

Mr. Walker bounded aboard the wagon in a single leap.

"Have you ever known anyone to be mauled by a kitten?"

"Where there's a cub, there's a mother cat."

"Not this time. It was an orphan and you frightened the life out of it."

"Reckon you didn't notice that Mama was about to leap down on your head."

"Surely not!" Shocked, her mouth sagged open. A shiver trembled through her, scalp to toe.

"Creeping across the branch over your head."

She ought to say something in self-defense but she couldn't imagine what.

"Hold on tight. That's one angry predator."

He cracked a whip in the air several inches over the team's heads. The wagon jolted and she clutched the coffee bag to keep from tumbling backward.

The horses raced down the path. She glanced back.

The cougar followed for a short distance then turned back, probably to tend to her cowering baby.

Screech, his cage tucked between a bag of flour and a crate, fell off his perch, squawking in a panicked flash of green feathers.

Huddled beside the campfire and staring silently at the flames, Miss Moreland seemed to be contrite.

He couldn't be sure, though. From what he had seen of her so far, contrition would not be something that came naturally.

Could be she was too cold to say anything. Possibly the shivering kept whatever was on her mind locked in her head.

The blamed woman had objected to removing her clothing and letting it dry by the fire like any sensible person would do, even though he had offered his oiled canvas to cover her.

It had taken his comment about her lips turning blue for her to do the smart thing and dry her clothes, the outer ones, anyway.

She wasn't unintelligent as far as he could tell, which had to mean she was stubborn.

That might not be a bad thing. She'd need some stubborn to make it in Montana since she seemed to be lacking in good sense.

Even little children knew to give a wide berth to a cougar cub.

He'd do his duty and see Miss Moreland safely to Hershal. After that it would be up to the old man to make sure she survived.

A wildcat's cry cut the dusk.

Miss Moreland glanced at him across the fire, her eyes widening in fear. At least he hoped it was fear.

"That won't be your cat, Miss Moreland."

She breathed out a short huff of relief. That, and the way her shoulders slumped, made him want to comfort her.

Of all the things he wanted to be feeling, sympathy wasn't one.

With a grunt to indicate his displeasure, he got up and crossed to her side of the fire. He sat down beside her.

"My last name is Lane," she murmured.

Why was that? he couldn't help but wonder. Couldn't say that it didn't make him uneasy. An unmarried lady ought to be carrying her family name of Moreland.

As it was, an unmarried woman coming to this part of the country all alone made him uneasy. No doubt, she wanted something from Hershal.

Moreland Ranch was a prime piece of property. With the railroad on the way, bringing settlers by the hundreds, the ranch would be sought after. With all the building that would be going on, the trees alone would be worth more than gold.

It was possible that Miss Lane had only good intentions, but it was his job to be suspect.

For three years Hershal had been writing, asking the girl to come to see him, and for three years she hadn't. So why now when the ranch and its resources had become so valuable?

His boss paid him generously to look after the spread, making sure the cattle were cared for and the buildings well kept.

Years ago, when Lantree had felt like a ship lost at sea, Hershal had listened to his story, then offered him a home and a job. In doing that, he had given him back his self-respect.

He would protect the old man, be it from the greedy mayor of Coulson or the lovely Miss Lane.

"I can't help but wonder why you don't carry your family name." He probably shouldn't have stated that so boldly, but there it was. *Let's see if she gives an honest answer.*

"It's the name my aunt Eunice gave me." She glanced at him with eyes the color of an ocean wave. Then she stared into the fire, silent for a long time.

Not dishonest, but vague.

"Why have you come here, Miss Lane?"

"To get to know my grandfather, of course."

She continued to stare at the fire and apparently did not notice that the canvas wrapped about her gaped open at her chest.

Her under-things were fine, lacy and frilly… and sheer with the dampness. He was ashamed of himself for letting his gaze linger.

For all that he didn't trust her, she was finely formed.

"Mr. Walker." She looked at him suddenly, catching him peering where he had no right to.

Dark brows lowered over dark-lashed eyes. The campfire cast her high cheekbones in shades of pink. She yanked the canvas tight across her charms.

"I beg your pardon, Miss Lane." He'd never considered himself a rude man and was humiliated to find that trait within him.

"If you are a man of honor, let me make one thing clear." Until a moment ago he'd believed he was. "I do not wish to be courted. I am a spinster and accepting of my fate. I would not welcome any action that would dissuade me from that future."

"Again, I do beg your pardon." No wonder she thought he had wooing on his mind, the way he had been staring.

"I should warn you," she said, ignoring his apology. "If you are not a man of honor, I do not take dalliances lightly. There is a man back in Kansas City who presumed that I did. I'm quite sure he is still being laughed at today."

As pretty as Miss Lane was, she was stiff. He would believe that she had a heart as cold as winter if he hadn't shared a bout of laughter with her and seen her concern for the cougar cub.

He couldn't help but wonder how she would act with Hershal. He'd have to be on guard to make sure she didn't wound his kind old heart.

"You can believe this or not, but until this moment, I have been respectful of women. I humbly ask for your forgiveness."

"Forgiveness granted." She smiled at him all of a sudden, brightly with her white teeth flashing. It nearly knocked him flat, which was something given that he was already sitting on the ground. "By George, that gives me one apology to your two."

He laughed. How could he help it?

"I hope you don't mind my saying so," she said. "But your smile is ever so much nicer than your scowl."

The fact was, she made him want to smile, and not for the first time.

But no matter how charming she might seem, he did not know her. He feared what she might be up to.

At least, with her being an avowed spinster, he didn't need to worry about losing his heart to her…because he could not swear that, in spite of everything, it would not happen. From what he'd glimpsed, she had a body to make a man daydream.

Hell damn him as an idiot for letting his mind wander there. He was a confirmed bachelor as much as she was a confirmed spinster.

A woman needed a secure future where she could put down roots…children needed the same. It made his blood run cold thinking of the things that might happen to them. Children needed to live closer to town…to be near a competent doctor in case of an emergency. These days he was a far better cowboy than he was a doctor.

"Can you tell me what my grandfather is like?"

The quick change in the conversation made

him uncomfortable. He didn't want to tell her who the old man was. If he did, she could more easily make plans to do whatever it was she intended.

"He's a cold man. Not really open to shows of affection." He shook his head slowly. "Likes to keep to himself mostly. The cabin is small. Surely not up to a lady's standards. Things could be uncomfortable for you."

She nodded, as though she had expected as much.

"He didn't seem cold in his letters."

He felt ashamed all of a sudden. He could tell by the look in her eyes that she believed him. No hope for it now but to carry on.

"Is it possible that he is only reserved?" she said. "I've known folks like that. What seems cold only hides a warm heart."

"That's not him."

"Surely he's generous, though. He did send me the violin. It had to have been precious to him."

"That's not the reason he sent it." He hated himself right now. "Your grandmother was always playing the thing, he told me. To him it was all a bunch of screeching—your bird ought to remind him of her playing. When she died he wanted to get rid of it, but didn't feel right throwing it out. So he sent it to you."

She bowed her head, covered her face with her hands, silent for a long time.

When she looked up her eyes were moist.

"That's not what… Well, thank you for telling me… I believe my dress is dry. I'll just step into the trees for a moment."

She gathered the canvas about her and walked toward the darkness beyond the fire. She hesitated, then stepped beyond his sight.

Reaching for the Winchester that he always kept close at hand, he cocked his head, listening for danger over the shuffling of fabric.

It wasn't easy to admit that it might not be the wild things that were the biggest threat to her, but that he was.

Clearly his lie about the violin had crushed her. He had heard her play and knew very well that she had a gift…a gift that had been passed down from Catherine Moreland.

Could be that she really did want to simply meet her granddaddy, make the old man's life better.

The trouble was, at this point, he wasn't ready to take that risk.

He would be watching her, morning and night.

It would be a sorry day that he allowed anyone to harm Hershal Moreland.

Rebecca sat astride the bag of coffee beans with her knees bracing the sides. She tucked her violin under her chin then poised the bow over the strings.

After a day of the wagon jouncing over rocks and slamming into ruts along the narrow path, her stomach felt unsettled.

Poor Screech must have had half of his feathers bent with the jostling he had taken. As soon as they reached the safety of the cabin, she would make him a perch and let him out of his cage.

Mr. Lantree had estimated that, bears, cougars, storms and floods notwithstanding, they should arrive at her grandfather's humble cabin before sunset.

That happy event could not come soon enough. For the past three hours Mr. Walker had been preaching about the hardships of life on the ranch, the constant danger and her grandfather's thorny character.

In her opinion, Grandfather could not possibly be thornier than the man currently whistling some sort of command to the horses.

If he was, this trip will have proven something

that she did not want to know. That Aunt Eunice had been right and there was no such thing as a good Moreland.

She would not let her mind dwell on the fact that she was half Moreland.

How odd that in Grandfather's letters he came across as congenial. She would not have made this long, perilous trip had she believed that he had no desire for a loving relationship with her.

To lift her spirits she had, at great risk of falling from the wagon, rummaged through her belongings and taken out her violin.

She drew the bow across the strings but because one of the rear wagon wheels bounced in a rut, what should have been a lovely note was delivered as a squeal.

All of a sudden the wagon slowed, inching gently over the path.

To some folks, communing with a dead man would be odd. To Rebecca it was normal…comforting in fact.

Yes, by George, even from beyond the grave, Mr. Mozart was better company than Mr. Walker, whose clean blond hair caught the sunlight as he sat tall on the wagon bench.

She closed her eyes and let Mozart and…she would not believe this was not true in spite of what Mr. Walker had to say…her grandmother guide the bow across the strings. "Eine kleine Nachtmusik" took her to a happy place where her grandfather embraced her and her escort smiled.

When she finished the piece, she noticed that the wagon had stopped. She opened her eyes to find Mr. Blond-Haired Viking turned about on the bench. To her great surprise, he was smiling.

"I wonder if these trees have ever heard Mozart," he said quite pleasantly.

She would not have guessed that he was familiar with the composer. The man was certainly a puzzle…one that she would not be solving.

"They'll be hearing a lot more of it, I guess. From what you have told me about my grandfather, he won't be pleased to have me playing in the cabin."

"I reckon not," he said, his customary frown settling back into place.

He turned, clicked to the team then mumbled something under his breath.

She thought it was "Damned shame."

Many things in life were. One could only face them and hope for the best.

If she had to escape into the pristine forest to visit her composer friends and feel her grandmother's hand glide along with hers, there were worse places to be.

As long as one was not crushed by a rolling boulder or attacked by displaced snakes.

Chapter Five

"Welcome home, Miss Lane," Mr. Walker stated.

If he expected an answer, she could not find the words—or the breath, for that matter—to respond.

They had stopped at the top of a hill, and gazing down she didn't believe there was a place on Earth that could be more beautiful.

In the distance the sky, the most pure shade of blue she had ever seen, met a snowcapped mountain range. The mountain looked rocky, forbidding and altogether magnificent. About halfway down, the rocks gave place to tall green trees. Lower down, the trees became less dense, with verdant meadows claiming space among them as the land flattened out.

"Look close." He pointed his finger at the valley below. "You can just make out Big Timber

Creek. It cuts through the ranch. Half the acreage is on one side and half on the other. Your grandfather also owns a few hundred acres on the south side of the Yellowstone. The nearest neighbor is a half a day's ride away."

"I wish… Oh, never mind." What she wanted was impossible, so why put it out there for Mr. Walker to make fun of?

"You wish you hadn't come to this isolated place after all, I reckon. Just say the word and I'll see you on the next riverboat out of Coulson."

"That's kind of you," she said, understanding full well that it was not kindness motivating him. Clearly, he did not want her here. "But that's not what I was going to wish for."

"Wishes have their place, but out here it's hard work that counts for something."

As if she knew nothing of hard work. Aunt Eunice had gone to pains to make sure her girls did not grow up to be ornaments.

"What I wished, was that I could put this to music." She swept her arm at the paradise displayed before her eyes. "To capture it on my violin. But, by the saints, I could try for a hundred years and never get it right."

She could not read his expression. He stared at her, silent for a long moment.

"I don't know that anyone's ever tried."

Well, that was something. He had not ridiculed her after all.

"If you look hard you can just make out the ranch house and the outbuildings. There's the big barn off to the left and down a ways."

The barn was easy to spot, being red. The other three buildings were brown, probably made of logs. Two of them were small...but the other?

Even from this distance she could see that the main house was huge, two stories high with what appeared to be a porch all around the ground level.

If this was Mr. Walker's idea of a cramped cabin, well—

"If we hurry, we ought to make it home by sundown," he said, disrupting her opinion of his judgment.

Smoke curled out of the chimney of one of the small cabins. It whisked away out of four chimneys of the main house.

Even though it was only four o'clock, the evening chill was beginning to set in. Seeing the little settlement, Rebecca was suddenly anxious for the safety of four walls.

It would be wonderful to lay her head down

tonight without having to peer into the darkness, fearful of eyes staring back from the bushes.

Even if her grandfather did not welcome her, if he made her sleep in the barn, she would snuggle next to some docile, furry creature and sleep soundly.

The lamps in the main house and the bunkhouse had already been lit when Lantree pulled the wagon into the yard. Flowers in the flower beds on both sides of the porch had already closed their petals to the coming night. Three dogs on a rug near the front door wagged their tails in welcome.

As usual he was nervous coming home after an absence. Any number of things could have gone wrong.

While Hershal was capable, the limitations of age were starting to show. He wasn't as agile as he had been when Lantree had first met him. He forgot things now and again and he took more naps.

His voice was still as booming as ever, though. His word was still law.

Everything seemed calm this evening…and it's not as though there were not competent hands working the ranch. It's just that none of them would even know how to tend a blister. Lantree at least could still do that along with some other minor treatments.

There was the big, congenial ranch hand, Tom Camp. The man was good at following directions. Tom would do whatever was asked of him and do it well. Loyal by nature, he was a good friend.

There was also Jeeter Spruce, but he was young and impatient to earn enough money to strike out on his own.

Lastly, there was Barstow, who did not own up to a last name. No one minded that because he cooked the best vittles in the territory. Barstow had no interest in running anything but the kitchen.

Now, there was the granddaughter.

He'd feel easier in himself if he thought she had the ranch's best interest at heart.

Once she inherited, and he figured she would, she might sell the place. If she didn't do that, she might cut down the trees, rape the land and break the old man's heart.

Moreland cared for trees more than most folks did. He believed that because they were integral to the natural beauty of the land, a home for wildlife and had been a rightful part of the environment long before there had been a Moreland Ranch, they had earned the right to keep their roots in Montana's rich earth.

Even if those were not his beliefs, it had been Mrs. Moreland's dying wish to preserve them.

Anyone who threatened a tree threatened the beloved memory of Catherine Rose Moreland.

Respecting her memory meant respecting her trees.

Cattle rustlers were expected and tolerated, to an extent. More than once Moreland turned a blind eye if he knew the rustlers to be hungry. The same could not be said for the riverboat folks in need of fuel and the railroad men in need of tracks.

It wasn't as though Moreland's trees were the only ones about. The mountains were full of them. But his timber held the most appeal, given that his forests were near the river.

He'd lost track of the times his boss had sent Mayor Smothers's lackeys running for home, fearing for life and limb…and sanity.

"I'm fairly certain," Miss Lane said, bringing him back to the issues of the moment, "that you called this great, lovely home a cramped cabin."

Yes, he had told her that. He'd told her many things that were not true. One by one he was

sure to be called on them. It wouldn't be long
before he would have to deal with his misrepre-
sentations about Hershal Moreland's character.

The old man was sure to have something to
say about that.

All of a sudden a gunshot exploded from inside the barn, saving him from having to answer
to his lie that very moment.

He took off at a run, leaving Miss Lane to
find her own way off the wagon. A gun being
fired from inside the barn could only mean that
Hershal had captured a tree rustler.

"What do you make of that, Screech?"

The bird, being unused to gunfire, had fallen
from his perch with a thump, then righted himself with an outraged fluff of green feathers.

"Uh-oh," he stated then used his hooked beak
to climb the bars to his perch.

"Well, by the saints, I will not sit here like
an abandoned ninny." She eyed the drop to the
ground, grateful for once for every inch of her
six feet.

She stood up and turned away from the buck-
board. Cautiously, she felt for a foothold. Finding one, she lowered herself down, then felt for
the next spot to anchor her toe.

Luckily, she was good at getting out of wagons unassisted. The last thing she wanted to do was break or twist a limb…to seem inept in front of her grandfather.

And, she could only admit, it would be the humiliation to end all if Mr. Walker found her sprawled on the ground unable to rise.

After a moment, having met with only one slippery mishap, she set both feet on solid ground.

But what to do now? Go into the house uninvited? Worse, go into the barn uninvited and maybe get shot?

One thing was for certain, she was not going to stand here shivering in the cold with the darkness growing more dense by the moment.

"I'm going to follow Mr. Walker," she called to Screech.

Really, there was nothing else to do. He was the only person she knew. In spite of his negative attitude, she did feel a sense of security in his large presence.

Creeping up to the closed barn door, she listened to the voices inside, still not convinced she ought to enter.

"You see that portrait hanging below the loft?" an elderly-sounding voice bellowed. It nearly shivered the timbers of the door. "That's my Catherine Rose."

Her grandfather! It had to be.

The portrait must be of her grandmother. She would give anything to see an image of her mentor.

"I do see it, sir," came a voice, this one young and sounding fearful.

"Before she died she charged me with guarding her trees. I carry that obligation close to my heart. Promised I'd shoot anyone who cut one of them down."

"He's young for shooting," she heard Mr. Walker say, his voice sounding casual. "Maybe you ought to send him home in the dark."

"Shooting would be kinder, Lantree. My wife's ghost has been known to scar a man for life."

Lantree...she liked that name. She would enjoy using it if she and Mr. Walker ever became friendly enough for that familiarity.

"It's got to be against the law, shooting somebody over a tree," the young voice declared, but with a quaver. "And I don't believe in ghosts."

"Look hard at the face in the portrait, boy. Hers is not one you want to meet in the dark, especially when she's riled. Those eyes look scary now, but when they fill up with blood… Well, son, you don't want to see it."

She'd learned something about her grandfather already. He stretched the truth…and quite possibly, he was a bully. And very clearly he set great store by trees.

"I reckon I won't shoot you." Her grandfather's voice dripped with regret. "As long as you deliver a message to that scallywag Smothers."

"The mayor?" The young man sounded surprised.

"Don't play dumb." This from Lantree Walker. "You are working for him."

"I'm only building a house for me and my bride." He sounded sincere to her.

"I reckon he's lying, don't you, Lantree?"

"Shifty eyes say he is."

"If my eyes are shifting it's because I'm looking back and forth between the two of you and that snake-haired thing on the wall."

"Snake? Wouldn't insult the late missus if I were you. You'll only feel her eyes on your back when you hightail it back to town."

"I ain't going to Coulson."

"Why should we believe that?" said Lantree Walker.

She really did like his name. She would no

longer call him Mr. Walker, in her mind at any rate.

"Because I know things."

"And, as an offer of good faith, you'll share them with us." This from Grandfather.

"Could be. If you'll call off your dead wife. Let me go home to mine in peace."

So, he did believe in ghosts after all.

A cold breeze stroked the back of her neck. She did not believe in ghosts, but that would not keep her from looking over her shoulder if she were walking through the woods tonight.

"Catherine Rose says she'll stay in her portrait if you have something important to share…and if you keep your saw off her trees."

"I do know something about Smothers. I'm not involved, but I was approached. Only because of my size, mind you. The mayor is looking for big men—poachers, you'd call them—to go after your trees. The ones close to the river so they can get in and out during the night real fast like, so as you won't notice."

"Smothers wants to build a whole town. I reckon we'd notice," Lantree Walker said.

There was silence for a time, then some rustling. She desperately wanted to go inside the barn and see what was happening.

She pressed her ear closer to the door.

"Let's have a look at that bruised eye," Lantree said, his voice sounding softer all of a sudden.

She turned her head, listening with her other ear.

"No permanent damage. It will be colorful for a time, though."

"You a doc or something?"

All at once the barn door opened inward. She lost her balance and stumbled forward.

Praise all the saints, she did not go down. She righted herself and with as much dignity as she could manage under the circumstances, she faced her grandfather.

White eyebrows slanted downward over blue eyes. White hair stuck out at angles on top of his head as though he had been yanking it.

The tree thief inched along the sidewall of the barn.

"Lantree," her grandfather said, his frown softening while he looked at her face, "did you take my advice and finally marry a wife?"

"I've been gone all four days. Where would I get a bride in that amount of time?"

"Coulson, where else? She does look gently used."

By the saints!

"I have not been used at all," she declared with a proper lift of her chin.

Apparently, her actual occupation was something that she would have to make clear to every male she met in these mountains. Perhaps she would take to wearing a needle and thread in her collar permanently.

By George, was there a woman in Coulson who was not a professional giver of comfort?

"She's not my wife."

"Why then did you bring her here?"

Her grandfather peered closely up at her, his expression slowly changing from curiosity to astonishment.

"Are you… No… But I think… Could you really be…?"

He reached for her face, as though he wanted to touch her, then he dropped his hand to his side. His eyes moistened.

Perhaps he recognized someone in her. His son…or his wife.

She glanced at the portrait they had used to scare the thief.

By George, she had been traveling for some time, but she hoped she did not look like Medusa, with snakes growing out of her head instead of hair.

The captive had inched his way to within three feet of the barn door.

"Hershal, this is Rebecca Lane, your granddaughter." Lantree made the introduction, although she was sure that at this point it was unnecessary.

The tree-napper rushed out of the barn, into the dark.

If he was foolish enough to believe that the portrait in the barn was the late Mrs. Moreland, she could only say heaven help him on his long run home to his wife...or to Coulson.

"Of course it is. I should have known. It's like I've seen a ghost."

Oh, my. She couldn't help glancing once more at the portrait. Rebecca was no beauty, but surely—

"A lovely vision of my past, is what I meant, Rebecca. That—" he indicated the portrait with a nod of his white head "—is to scare trespassers."

Her grandfather opened his arms, clearly waiting for her to rush into them.

She glanced at Lantree, who was staring at the barn floor, nudging a pebble with the toe of his boot.

Apparently, Grandfather was coldhearted

in the same way that the house was a cramped cabin.

"I know I'm a stranger to you, Rebecca, but to me you are—" His eyes glittered.

Family, she knew he meant. She felt it, too.

She stepped into his embrace gently when she wanted to launch into it. She was not a tiny thing and he was an old man…not frail, but not robust, either.

For all that they were strangers, there was a bond between them.

Her name was Catherine Rose.

Lantree walked up the front porch steps behind Hershal and Miss Lane, carrying the birdcage in his left hand and a large bag of flour under his right arm. Barstow always wanted his flour first thing on coming back from town.

His boss grinned up at his granddaughter and she smiled down at him. Chances are she was walking into his heart as neatly as she was his home.

That could be dangerous. Then again, she might be just the person to bring joy to his sundown years.

Coming across the threshold, Lantree paused

to look at the familiar portrait hanging over the mantel.

The lady gazing down had been older than Miss Lane when the portrait was painted. Still, the high cheekbones were the same...the eyes an exact match in color. No, he thought as he studied the painting, the resemblance was more than mere pigment. The artist had captured an expression, an angle of the chin and an arch of the brow that was common to both women.

If Miss Lane hadn't knocked the sense out of him that first night, he might have recognized her then.

Watching the old man stop ten paces into the main room of the log house then turn to kiss his granddaughter's cheek, Lantree could only imagine the emotion brewing behind his grin.

Joy, certainly, but more than that, he sensed that Hershal felt he had been granted a miracle.

They had all talked about Rebecca Lane coming one day, but it had been castles in the sky. No one, except maybe Hershal, had expected her to actually walk in the front door.

In the end he had to look away from them because he felt like an intruder on a very private moment.

He didn't like feeling like an intruder where his boss was concerned.

Until Miss Lane had stumbled her tall, lovely self into the barn, he had felt like a son to Hershal. They had grown that bond between them over the years.

Now, here stood the real kin, wiping tears from her cheeks…and his.

"It's about time you got home from Coulson!" Barstow's voice bellowed from out of sight.

Heavy footsteps pounded down the hallway leading from the kitchen. Hearing him come down the hall one would guess that the cook was a giant of a man. But he stood only five feet tall, and was half that much around the middle.

"Haven't baked a pie in an age!" He rounded the corner, his large nose leading the way. He stopped abruptly, nearly stumbling over his small feet.

Hershal let go of his granddaughter and pivoted toward Barstow.

"Bake six!" he exclaimed. "One for each of us."

Hell and damn if Hershal hadn't just killed the fatted calf. Extravagance was rare in the mountains since restocking supplies meant a week-long trip to town.

"Strike me bald!" Barstow waddled across the room. He caught up Miss Lane's hands in his, lifted one and kissed her fingertips. "You can only be our Rebecca."

Did it really take one minute for a stranger to become "our Rebecca"?

"You are your grandmother stepped off her portrait," Barstow said, then sniffled.

The cook had been with Hershal for thirty-five years, going with him from city, to country, then finally here to the wilds of Montana.

Lantree set the birdcage on the hearth in front of the softly glowing fire. The feathered critter was shivering and, for once, silent.

"Lantree," Barstow ordered, "bring in our Rebecca's things while I trot upstairs and ready her a room."

That would be something to see, Barstow trotting. Sometimes the lamp shades trembled when he crossed the room.

"What is that?" The cook halted with one hand on the banister and one foot poised in the air. He stared at the birdcage.

"Not a green chicken!" Miss Lane hurried toward the hearth and opened the cage door. "Come on out."

Screech cocked his head from side to side, seeming to consider the wisdom of such a move.

Rebecca puckered her mouth and made loud kissing noises to coax the bird out.

He ought to look away, but how could he? No man with healthy red blood thrumming in his veins could.

He blinked, shook his head.

She kissed the air again.

Backing toward the front door, he squeezed his eyes shut, but that didn't do a damned thing to block out the moist smacking sounds.

"Isn't that…" he heard Hershal ask.

"Couldn't be… Not possible," Barstow answered.

He opened his eyes to see the bird perched on Miss Lane's arm and Barstow approaching one slow, cautious step at a time.

"Looks like him," Hershal said.

"All birds of his species look like him," Barstow answered, scratching his head of thick black hair. "But may I ask where you came by him?"

"He was with me when my mother left me with my aunt. I guess we've had each other all our lives."

"Was he ever called Kiwi Clyde, do you

know?" Barstow asked, his face beginning to look eager.

Barstow had mentioned his bird many times. It seemed that the cook had never really gotten over Hershal's son stealing his feathered friend when he ran away from home so many years ago.

From what Lantree could tell, the absence of Kiwi Clyde had been felt more sorrowfully than the absence of the son.

Of course, the bird had not chosen to leave and, as the story went, the son had snuck away, stealing a great deal of money along with the bird.

"Aunt Eunice always called him Screech because, well...you'll come to find that he excels at it."

"A screecher, eh? I'd bet that bird is our Kiwi Clyde," Hershal insisted. "Little Kiwi Clyde was Barstow's bird. My son made off with him in a coldhearted way...but that's the way the boy was. We can talk about him later if there's things you want to know, but for now we need to prove that Screech used to be Kiwi Clyde."

"Can't figure how you'll do that," Lantree observed.

"Did you remember the peppermint sticks from town?"

"I sure did, just like you said."

Barstow clapped his hands together. "Go fetch them, son, we'll know soon enough."

In going out the door, he passed close by Miss Lane. Her womanly scent caught him in the gut, turning him every which way of uneasy.

He'd been around women, professionally and personally, but not even his fiancée had made him react in such a primal way.

Could be it was Miss Lane's size. He considered the possibility while he dug through a canvas bag for the peppermint.

He huffed out a breath, knowing that was not the case. It had always taken more than physical perfection to arouse him.

Dallying with women was not something he took lightly.

By and large, sweet, feminine ladies were tiny things. His fiancée had been only five feet three inches tall.

During intimate moments he had always held back. Hell, he could never let down his guard and get lost in the passion for fear of injuring her.

There wasn't much satisfaction in indulging in an act that might result in injury.

At least physically, Moreland's precious

granddaughter was his match. In part, that's what had him riled up down below, but not all.

Maybe if he— But no… Serious commitment, and that was the only kind he wanted, was not for him.

He grabbed the peppermint sticks then took the porch stairs two at a time. It didn't matter how tall Miss Lane was, she was a declared spinster and he was an avowed bachelor. And that's how things needed to remain.

He strode into the house to find Barstow scratching the bird's neck.

Funny, he never knew birds liked that. This one seemed to be in a pleasure trance.

"Here we are!" Moreland strode forward and plucked a peppermint stick from his hand. "We'll soon know if this is our boy."

"Clydie want a candy?" Hershal asked.

The bird snapped out of his trance. His pupils flared.

"Here, yummy!" Bumbling instead of graceful, the bird flew from Miss Lane to Hershal.

"Mmm yummy! Here!"

Barstow plucked the candy away from Hershal and held it before the bird.

With a squawk, he snatched it, and then curled his toes around the treat. The critter seemed happy enough, nibbling and making contented sounds.

"Do you give him peppermint often?" Barstow looked at Rebecca, clearly hoping that the answer would be no. That the reunion with the treat would prove that this was his lost bird.

"No, never. Aunt Eunice would not have permitted it." Miss Lane arched a fine brow. She smiled. "It's quite clear to me that Screech can only be your Kiwi Clyde."

The bird was lost in bliss. Barstow was lost in bliss.

If this was not the missing bird, no one was going to say so.

Hershal clapped one open hand on his chest. "I say call the others in from the bunkhouse, open a bottle of wine and we'll give three cheers to Rebecca and Kiwi Clyde's homecoming."

Lantree would make that toast but he'd only give two cheers. The last he'd hold in reserve until he knew that Miss Rebecca Lane meant no harm.

Chapter Six

Rain tapped on the window beside Rebecca's bed. She watched while a drip rolled down the pane. It caught a companion then together they rushed down the glass. For some reason this reminded her of happy times with Melinda.

She hadn't expected to be homesick. Although it wasn't that she missed home so much as she missed her cousin.

There was so much she wanted to share with Melinda. If only she could send a mental message to her, the way they had practiced doing as children.

She closed her eyes tight, pictured her cousin in her mind, then concentrated on three images.

The first was of the nights she had spent sleeping on the lower deck of the *River Queen*. In the beginning, bedding down in the open with livestock and feedbags for company had been adventurous. The boat's rocking and the noise of the steam engine had lulled her to sleep. Later on, the engine just sounded loud and the constant rocking was not pleasant. Still, she always had a lovely view of God's great starry canopy. And she never had grown tired of the sound of the water slapping the side of the boat.

Next, she sent images of the nights she had spent sleeping on the ground close to the campfire. She had kept Screech, now known as Kiwi Clyde, tucked close to her at all times for fear that something would creep out of the darkness and snatch him. The same as on the boat, there had been the stars, constant and beautiful.

Tonight, she couldn't see the stars because of the rain.

Glancing about the bedroom at its small hearth and its comfortable furnishings, she sent Melinda an image of security. No roaming cats or marauding bears would breach the sanctuary of good, solid logs.

Just now, beyond the thrum of the rain on the glass, she heard a wolf howl. Another wolf answered, this one closer to the house. She snuggled into her blanket.

There was one more image she nearly sent… but caught it back. This image was for her alone.

There had been a moment on the trail to the ranch when early in the morning she had come upon Lantree Walker kneeling beside a stream. His back was to her and she only glimpsed him through a stand of trees, but he had taken off his shirt while he splashed cold water on his face and upper body.

Muscles flexed, early-morning light glinted off his skin… She'd looked away, but not before the image was scorched behind her eyes.

With a sigh, she flung the covers off her bed. Why was the room so hot all of a sudden? The fire in the hearth was nothing more than a glow.

Getting up, she put on her robe and decided to check on Screech. Grandfather and Barstow had constructed a perch for him near the fireplace in the great room, just like the one he used to sit upon when he was but a chick.

It would make him feel at home, since that was his familiar place, she had been assured. But if he had been used to wolves howling in the night, it had been a very long time ago.

Even though the floor was cool, she didn't bother with slippers. Grandfather and Barstow, the only men of the ranch to live in the main house, had gone to bed hours ago.

The hands, Tom and Jeeter, lived in the bunk-house down the hill, closer to the barn.

Lantree Walker lived in a cabin of his own nearer the house. It was in clear view of her bedroom window.

Coming down the stairs, she heard a rustling from below.

In spite of the reassurances, Screech was, no doubt, unsettled in his new surroundings.

Not that the surroundings were not beautiful. The main room was huge, with three fireplaces to warm it. One beside the dining table, one near the front door and the other along the back wall. This one was as tall as a man and had five comfortable chairs set in front of it, one chair for each man on the ranch. From what she had gathered, it was customary for the five of them to pass the evening hours together.

The house smelled good, too, like beeswax. That must be why the log walls gleamed.

She hurried down the hall and made a quick turn into the big room.

"Oh, hello," she said, coming to a sudden halt three steps inside the room.

Good glory! She was not decently dressed for socializing. Her sleeping gown was sheer, her ruffled robe far from prudish. Mentally, she gave herself a kick in the rump for not taking a moment to put on her slippers. It would be good to remember that she no longer lived in a house with only females.

"Good evening, Miss Lane."

Lantree Walker glanced at her, but briefly. He returned his attention to a sixth chair that he was placing before the fireplace.

"This one is for you."

"Well, I thank you." She pinched the inadequate robe closed under her chin. "That's very kind."

"No need to thank me. This was your grandfather's doing. He had this made special for you. Here," he said, indicating the padded chair with a sweep of his big hand. "Come and try it out."

"Well, I…" This was quite improper, but perhaps the social rules in Montana were different from those in Kansas City.

"Don't be shy."

He smiled at her so she crossed the room then sat down.

"This is lovely." She wriggled into the big stuffed cushions. "It's a comfortable fit. Not all chairs are."

He sat down in the chair next to her…his chair

she guessed, since it was even larger than the one she sat in.

He stared at the orange embers in the fireplace for a moment, silent and seeming to forget her presence.

"I'm glad it's a fit," he said at last. "It was no easy task getting it all the way from Coulson without a scratch or rip."

"I'm confused."

He glanced fully at her. My, but he was handsome, with that long blond hair brushing his shoulders, those moody-looking blue eyes seeming to peer out from under slightly lowered brows.

A woman could nearly rethink her position on remaining unmarried. Nearly, but not quite.

"About the chair," she said, recovering from her reckless thoughts. "How did he have it made for me? I only arrived today. And how did he know to make it my size?"

"You may have only arrived today, but you've been in the old man's thoughts ever since he found out about you. This chair was ordered more than a year ago."

"By the saints," she murmured.

At his smile, a chill skittered over her skin. A curiously warm chill.

Lantree—she would begin calling him that since she was on a first-name basis with everyone else on the ranch, so it would be awkward to not be so with him—folded his great muscular arms across his chest. Stretching out in his chair, he crossed his long legs at the ankle.

"The size of the chair was a wish on his part, that maybe you would take after Mrs. Moreland."

"Do I?" She wanted it desperately. To have that in common with her grandmother would be a gift beyond price.

"That's what I've been told. I never met the lady. She passed before I met your grandfather."

Raindrops pattered gently on the windows. She was beyond grateful that the journey from Coulson had not taken another day. As much as she enjoyed a storm, she preferred to enjoy it from indoors.

"Are you telling me the truth this time, Lantree?"

He arched a brow at her, seeming surprised.

"It's been some time since I heard my name coming from a woman's lips."

"I didn't mean to be forward, but everything is so different here. Life seems more casual. In Kansas City it's always Mr., Mrs. and Miss. I'd like for you to start calling me Rebecca."

He shot her a half smile.

"All right…Rebecca, I am being completely truthful. You do resemble your grandmother. All a body has to do is look at the portrait to see it."

Curse it! That statement just proved he was still lying, or at least giving the truth a very long stretch. Her grandmother had been an exceptionally desirable woman. She was not.

"There's something troubling me." She had to say so. "I can understand why you might have distrusted me at the start, given that you assumed I was a—" She waved her hand before her face, dismissing the word that she did not care to use in mixed company. "But later on, you deliberately misled me about my grandfather's character. I'd like to know why."

He returned his gaze to the coals, silent for so long she thought he would refuse to answer.

"I'll admit, I'd hoped to make you turn back. I care deeply for Hershal," he murmured, brooding at the orange glow in the hearth. "He helped me when I had no right to expect it. I figure I owe him my life. When I sense a threat, I protect him."

"And your highly tuned senses warn you I'm a threat?"

Silence again, then he sat up straight in his

chair and looked at her, his blue gaze sharp, judgmental.

"Why did you show up after all this time? I can't help but wonder. The old man's been waiting a long time. Now, all of a sudden, with the railroad coming and this property and its resources getting more valuable by the hour, here you are. Maybe you hope to inherit. I'd like to know the truth. Why did you come here?"

The man certainly had a greedy mind to assume such a thing. No doubt he was upset because he wanted to inherit and now he figured she had bumped him down the line.

By George, he would never get his greedy fingers on what was her grandfather's, not as long as she had a breath to breathe.

She stood up, shot his glare back at him.

The last thing she would tell him was that she had come in hopes of developing a family bond.

"I'm here because I didn't want to become the butcher's captive."

"I beg your pardon?" He looked confused but let him stay so.

"You may beg my pardon if you wish, but I do not give it to you." She spun about, copying Aunt Eunice's most practiced imitation of rebuff. "I bid you a good evening."

Just when she had nearly gained the sanctuary of the dim hallway his voice halted her, made her turn to gape at him.

"I can't help but wonder why a woman like you is not married. Surely there were a dozen men in Kansas City ready to rescue you from the butcher."

"What do you mean 'a woman like me'?"

"Beautiful…" He gestured with his hand, indicating her size, her shape.

"Sarcasm is never becoming," she muttered with her chin lifted a notch. She snatched her ruffled hem about her then turned to the hallway. When she was out of his sight, she ran for the sanctuary of her bedroom as fleetly as any five-foot beauty.

Early on the morning of a warm, crystal-skied day, Lantree saddled his horse, readying for a long day of checking the meadows for heifers ready to give birth. They needed to be brought into the paddock to keep them safe from predators.

While leading his horse out of the barn, a movement at the edge of the forest caught his eye.

Hell in a basket… There went Rebecca, her

strides confident yet graceful, walking into the forest…alone.

A week had passed since he had offended Hershal's granddaughter. Looking back on it, he could understand why she had been insulted. He'd questioned her motives regarding the old man.

What he could not figure out was why she got so riled up over being called beautiful. His former fiancée had basked in that type of compliment.

Over the past week, Rebecca had been polite to him while in Hershal's company, but stilted on the rare occasions that they found themselves alone.

He reckoned he had some silent treatment coming, given his suspicious attitude toward her.

The truth was, if she was up to no good, he couldn't see it. Just the opposite, Hershal all but glowed in her presence. He was eating better, sleeping more soundly and laughing more heartily.

And it wasn't only Hershal falling head over heels. All the men had become besotted over her to one degree or another.

Villain or saint, at this particular moment she

was up to some sort of foolishness, walking into the woods alone and taking the bird with her.

Looks like he'd have to ignore the calves for a bit and follow her. A female wandering in the mountains could only end up in trouble. Besides, believing that she was alone, she might say something to the bird, give up a secret that he ought to know about.

He gave her a five-minute head start. Long enough for her to believe that she was alone but not so far away that if she got into trouble, he would not be able to get to her in time to prevent a catastrophe.

It wouldn't be hard to find her, not with Kiwi Clyde riling up the native birds with his harsh squawking. Peace in the forest was being disturbed for miles around.

All of a sudden the parrot fell silent. For Hershal's and Barstow's sakes he hoped it had not been carried off by an eagle.

After trailing Rebecca for a mile, he spotted her kneeling in a meadow with yellow flowers sprouting all about the skirt of her blue-checkered gown.

The bird was out of his cage. Rebecca must not realize that there were dozens of meat-eaters that would soon be aware of the fact.

He stayed in the background watching…mesmerized, while she removed the pins from her hair then ran her hands through the rich-looking tresses tumbling down her back.

Sunshine glittered in the chestnut curls, turning them amber and gold.

If he weren't careful, she would snare him, just like she had the rest of the men on the ranch.

What he hadn't noticed when he spotted her going into the forest was that she had brought her violin along.

She removed it from its case then lifted it to her chin. Closing her eyes and raising her face to the sunshine, she began to play. A melody, sounding full of yearning—and at the same time, hope—washed over the meadow. She swayed with every draw of the bow across the strings.

The music filled him up, bathed his soul in peace and took him back to a time and place where he had not stood by, helpless against rampant disease. To a time when he had been in love, when he had made his living healing the hurting, and looked forward to a home of his own… to children.

In many ways that life had not been perfect, but the beautiful strains of the melody made him feel for the moment as if it had been.

When the piece was finished, she set the violin aside and opened her eyes. She sat down, looking skyward, she watched a big white cloud change shape as it blew across the mountaintop.

He ought to say something, let her know he was watching, but somehow, it seemed intrusive.

At last, she set the violin in its case then raised her hand into the air. She snapped her fingers.

Kiwi Clyde sailed out of a tree and perched on her arm. She drew him close to her face. The parrot nibbled her lips with his hooked bill.

She said something to the bird but from this distance he couldn't tell what.

For a moment, he wished he could be green and feathered, receiving kisses and sweet words.

Hell, what devilment had made him think that?

After a moment, Rebecca put the bird back in his cage. She stood, dusted grass and yellow petals from her skirt.

She walked the path back to the house, unaware that he was only steps away, hidden among the trees.

That worried him. A person in these parts needed to be aware of their surroundings, always cautious of what might be lurking in them. What was to say he could not have as easily been a wolf or a wildcat? Or worse…a trespasser.

For Hershal's sake, if not for Rebecca's own, he'd have to keep a close guard on her. Not that he could let her know it.

She appeared to be a lady of great independence. Ordinarily, that was a character trait that he admired. But mix it up in a womanly package and let her loose in the woods…that made him uneasy.

And while he was considering character traits, he could not overlook honesty. In all honesty, he would have to admit that he liked watching her walk.

Her long, bold strides and the sway of her hips intrigued him. He couldn't recall ever meeting a woman who possessed both size and feminine sweetness.

While he watched, she stopped, set down the violin and the bird then wound her hair into a neat bun. She jammed the pins back in.

Hell and damn. He was meant to live his life as a single man. All of a sudden he feared that he was going to need constant reminding. Maybe if he could continue to keep in mind that she might be up to no good, he would not fall under her spell.

He would remember this on rising and on falling asleep and every minute in between.

Still, once seen, the loveliness of those locks being warmed by sunshine and swaying with the heavenly music… Hell, there was no denying that it was a vision that would stay with him forever.

Rebecca smeared a dollop of beeswax on the long dining table then rubbed it to a shine with a square of cotton.

She smiled, satisfied with the renewed glow of the rich brown wood.

Doing chores came naturally to her. After a week of leisure, idle time had begun to chafe at her. There were only so many hours one could visit the office library or watch while Barstow prepared the meals. There were only so many questions she could ask the hands about their many duties before they became impatient with her.

Everyone on the ranch had a job to do and she was a woman used to being productive.

Having Grandfather treat her like she was a precious ornament made her feel useless.

It took some persuasion to convince him that a

woman could perform a chore and remain a lady. In the end he had allowed her to dust and polish.

His decision had been greeted with approval by the men since it freed them from taking turns doing a job that was, in all truth, foreign to their natures.

The front door slammed open and Jeeter rushed in, red in the face and breathing hard. The scent of an approaching storm blew in with him.

"Hershal!" he yelled.

Jeeter noticed her and tipped his hat.

"Good afternoon, Miss Rebecca," he said in a quieter tone.

"Good afternoon, Jeeter."

"Lantree's just brought in Fancy Francie!" he shouted to the house at large.

Footsteps hurried down the stairs. Lamps rattled with Barstow's rush from the kitchen.

"Who is Fancy Francie?" she asked while Jeeter fairly hopped from foot to foot.

"Why, she's our favorite cow, ready to calve."

Her grandfather hurried across the room, his cheeks flushed and his wide grin showing his excitement.

"Would you like to be there to greet the new calf?" he asked.

Maybe… She'd seen cats and dogs giving birth, even a mouse once, but a great big cow? It was bound to be a bloody, possibly painful process.

Left to her own desires, she would finish her dusting then visit the calf after it was safely delivered into the world. But there was nothing she would not do for the man she had become devoted to in such a short time.

Clearly, the term "blood ties" had its origins in fact. This bond that had sprung between her and her grandfather was as strong as the bond she felt for Melinda, whom she had known most of her life.

So she said, "I'd love to meet the new calf."

Jeeter dashed outside, long limbs churning across the yard in an awkward scramble.

Fancy Francie must have been a very special bovine to have everyone in such an uproar. Even Barstow sped past them toward the barn, his short legs stirring up the dust.

From the looks of the sky there wouldn't be dust much longer. Rain was coming and if the heavy black clouds were anything to go by, there would be a lot of it.

Inside the barn, lanterns were lit, giving the big building a soft amber glow.

"There's my good girl, Francie." Her grandfather hurried to the cow and laid his hand on her wide forehead. He stroked each of her brown ears then kissed the white spot between her eyes. "Everything is going to be just fine."

Barstow ran his hand across the cow's big, taut belly. "There will be a nice fat baby suckling you in no time at all."

During the short time that she had lived here, many cows had given birth, but none of them with this fanfare. Not to mention, they had all been nameless.

"Jeeter," she said to the young cowhand standing beside her. "Why is this cow so special?"

Fancy Francie seemed like a perfectly ordinary brown cow with big soft eyes. If there was anything fancy about her it was not in her appearance.

"She saved Hershal's life, is why." Jeeter blinked his blue, red-lashed eyes at her.

"Well, by George, that is extraordinary!"

"There's not a cow like her in all the world."

To her knowledge she had never heard of a cow saving a life.

"My word, how did she do that?"

"Fought off a bear and a cougar at the same time, then she pulled Hershal from waist-deep mud."

Men of the West were known for telling tall

tales. Clearly this had to be one. It would simply not be possible for a cow to do such a thing.

"Jeeter, I'm not that green. Really, how did she do it?"

"Old Hershal got himself stuck in the mud up to his hips going after Francie's calf. There was a bear eyeballing what was going on and it made our girl nervous. She set to bellowing so loud that it caught Lantree's attention. He galloped in to see Francie pawing the ground. She charged that big old bear. When Lantree fired his gun at a tree the bear took off like he had a bee up his butt."

She did know something about Lantree Walker shooting at trees.

"What about the cougar?"

"There probably was one. Whose to say? The gunshot blast would have sent it running, too."

She also knew something about cougars creeping along branches.

"And then Francie somehow pulled my grandfather from the mud?" She watched the cow pace about her stall, doubting this feat would even be possible.

"I swear it's the truth." Jeeter nodded his head, setting a mass of silky-looking red curls to jiggling. "Strike me dead if it ain't."

A clap of thunder rolled across the barn roof. Grandfather and Barstow glanced at Jeeter with concern.

"That's the truth, to an extent," Grandfather clarified. "She did pull me and her calf from the mud, but with the help of Lantree. He's the one lassoed me and the calf and urged Fancy to pull us out."

"Regardless of the details, it did happen," Barstow declared. "It's been decreed by Mr. Hershal and agreed on by us all, that none of her calves will fill a stew pot. Because of her service to the family she will never become a steak."

Fancy Francie let out a moo, long and sorrowful sounding. She lay down, but just for a moment. She struggled to her feet to pace the confines of her stall.

"Poor Francie," she murmured.

"Everything looks like it should," Hershal assured her. "Just give it an hour or two and you'll see the joy of motherhood glowing in her eyes. There's nothing quite as wonderful."

"Since everything looks normal," Barstow declared, "Jeeter and I will get back to our chores."

"I wouldn't mind staying," Jeeter put in.

"Reckon you wouldn't," Grandfather said. "But Lantree's still looking for heifers near their time. If you help him, he might get back before the storm hits."

With a hefty sigh of resignation Jeeter followed Barstow out of the barn.

Grandfather sat down on an overturned barrel. She sat beside him on another barrel a few inches shorter. This was nice. It put them at eye level.

"It's peaceful in here," she said. "Nice and cozy with the lamps making things look all mellow…and the sound of the wind blowing under the eaves."

"For us, but I don't know if Francie understands that. I worry that she will be spooked by the thunder… Makes it harder to do her job."

"I reckon nature knows the way, Grandfather, storm or not."

He nodded. "Most of the time that's true. And this is her third calf. It's just that she's a special girl."

Even knowing what she did about the cow's heroics, Fancy Francie looked perfectly ordinary.

"Grandfather," she said because they were alone, the barn was quiet, and she wondered if… "I just was wondering…did you ever meet my mother?"

He turned his concerned stare from Francie to

her. "I never did have that pleasure. I'd have liked nothing more though. I'm sure she was lovely."

"My memories see her as a doll, fair and pink-cheeked. Men always called her pretty...I remember that much. But as Aunt Eunice tells it, she was lovely in her appearance but Momma was a wild rose. She was a thorn in my aunt's side, even when they were growing up."

Grandfather nodded, his bushy white eyebrows drawn. "It's a hard thing, loving someone and watching them make wrong decisions."

"Aunt Eunice wasn't pleased when Momma came home, knocked on the door then pointed to me and Kiwi Clyde and declared that she could no longer care for us. Her husband—that's what she called him but Aunt Eunice never believed it—was gone and she didn't know where. Dead for all she knew."

"He wasn't dead, at least not then."

Her grandfather didn't look away while he spoke even though his eyes turned a moist blue. He took her hand in his large, rough fingers.

"He is now, though." He rubbed his thumb across her knuckles. "I reckon you want to know about your pa."

Did she? Not if he was as wicked as Aunt

Eunice said. Better to believe in the few fantasies she had spun about him.

"Only if it's not painful for you to talk about him."

"I reckon it will always be that, but Rebecca, having you here helps to make all the past ugliness make sense. Because without all of that, there wouldn't be you."

"My aunt, she holds on to resentments, and one of them is my papa. I'd like to know something better of him than what she had to say."

"Don't go thinking too harshly of your aunt. I'm sure she loved your mother and then along came a man who… Well, I'm sure Eunice was not all wrong in her opinion…and grief can be hard on the heart."

Grandfather took a long breath and let it out in a low hiss.

"Your father was a handsome little boy, always full of the dickens, but in a way that charmed. He learned to get his way with a smile or a laugh, even if what he wanted he shouldn't have had. Your grandmother was wise to his ways, but most folks liked to indulge him."

Grandfather stood up, stretched then walked to the barn door and looked out.

"It's beginning to rain," he announced, then returned to sit on the upended barrel. "He became spoiled, always getting what he wanted by conning others. The fact is, he might have gotten by in life, gone to Washington and become a politician, even. He was that much of a smooth talker. Well, when he was twelve years old, life gave him a turn."

From her stall, Francie gave a long moo which to Rebecca's mind sounded distressed.

"He had a close friend, a good boy from a fine family," Grandfather went on, apparently not overly concerned that anything might be wrong with his favorite cow. "One day the boys went to a swimming hole all the boys used to go to. No one much worried. I reckon we should have... Willie's friend got bit by a water moccasin. He got bit while tossing it away from Willie.

"Your father was never the same after that. Don't think that he was bad-natured, Rebecca. He just needed to be in control of everything and everyone. Well, he damn sure was not going to control me. He became a rebel to all authority. We knocked heads over everything. He ignored his mother's tears and my threats... Did whatever he pleased. One day when he was eighteen and we'd had a big set-to, he ran off with my sock money and the bird."

"That's when he met my mother, I suppose?"

He nodded. "A couple of years later. That is my understanding. I believe he did care for her."

"Aunt Eunice didn't think so. She swore they were both cursed."

"I don't believe that and you shouldn't, either." Grandfather glanced at the cow. She had begun to tremble. He frowned but continued to talk. "We're all just God's children with faults and virtues."

"Did you see him again?"

"Years later he came home to seek forgiveness...and to die."

In spite of the fact that she had never met her father, had only known him as that Moreland Devil, her heart ached. A lump swelled in her throat.

"I'm sorry, Grandfather." A man would still love his son even if they came to blows.

He nodded, she guessed, because he was also sorry.

"The boy was sick, run down from sinful living. He died in your grandmother's arms with her tears on his face. It was after that, that she took up the violin. Helped her cope, she said because she believed he could hear it on the other side. Until that time no one knew she had such a gift for music. Her playing was a comfort to us all."

"Did he know…" She almost couldn't say this past the lump in her throat. "What happened to my mother?"

He shook his head. "When you were born, he didn't want the responsibility so he lit out… He regretted it with his last breath, Rebecca. And I am sorry, but he didn't know anything about what had become of your mother."

"Aunt Eunice would say that Miss Francie was a better mother—" Something was happening in the stall. "Grandfather, I think the calf is coming!"

She leaped from the barrel and dashed to the stall.

"Look at those tiny hooves!" How astonishing! There was Francie, as normal looking as before but with a new life beginning to emerge from her body.

Grandfather spoke sweetly to his cow, using calm, soothing words.

"Rebecca, the calf's hooves are pointing up instead of down. It's breach. Find Barstow and have him fetch Lantree. I wouldn't ask you to go out in the rain but the situation is urgent."

Chapter Seven

Rebecca closed the barn door on Grandfather's string of cusswords. The cow was clearly in trouble.

Cold rain smattered her face and trickled down her scalp. She plucked up her skirt, tucked it in the crooks of her elbows then dashed toward the house, where Barstow was sure to be preparing supper.

How the cook would know where Lantree might be, she couldn't imagine. Barstow rarely left the house while Lantree spent most of his time outdoors.

But Grandfather had sent her to Barstow so she slogged her way through the mud.

A figure rounded the corner of the house. Jeeter seemed not to see her in his hurry to get out of the rain.

"Jeeter!" she called. "Have you seen Lantree?"

"In his cabin!"

The boy continued his dash to the bunkhouse, but too late to avoid the sudden downpour that suddenly crashed down on their heads.

Water dripped from her chin and her nose. Her progress toward Lantree's cabin was slow and slippery.

Visions of Fancy Francie, her calf's hooves facing the wrong way, chilled her. Her heart raced faster than her feet. She stopped to take off her boots. Stocking feet were bound to move more quickly than footwear that stuck to the earth like they were caked in gum.

Lantree's cabin was not far away. She spotted it nestled in a stand of trees, appearing blurry in the drenching rain.

It seemed to take forever but she arrived at the front steps. Stomping mud from her stockings, she crossed the porch then pounded on the door.

No response. She slammed her boots against the wood. Still no response.

By George, there was nothing for it but to act boldly. A cow and a calf depended upon her… lives hung in the balance!

She opened the door without invitation and stepped inside. Her feet left long smears of mud on the polished floor.

"Lantree…?" she called softly, feeling shy about invading his space.

Hopefully Jeeter had not been mistaken about him being here, but silence met her inquiry.

"Lantree Walker?" she called louder this time.

Whether he was home or not was something that she would not know until she searched every room. And circumstances being what they were, she absolutely had to know.

The cabin was small. He should not be hard to find. A quick glance told her that he was not in the bedroom. What a relief, she did not want to intrude upon him in that private space.

He was not in the cozily furnished main room of the house. The fire in the hearth had not been kindled.

If he was home, he had to be in the kitchen.

Safe enough. Surprising someone in the kitchen did not seem half as invasive as coming upon them in the bedroom.

And that would have been true had the kitchen not had a bathtub smack in the center…a bathtub with a naked Viking sprawled in it…who appeared to be deeply asleep.

She gawked at Lantree for a moment because her wits had scattered and she was helpless to do anything else.

His head lay back against the rim of the tub. His mouth was open, but just barely. The muscles of his neck flexed when he swallowed in his sleep.

Being a large man, the copper bathtub was not quite adequate to hold him. Great muscular arms hung over the sides. His fingers seemed relaxed with water still dripping from the tips. Long, powerful-looking legs draped over the tub lip, nearly touching the floor.

Any well-bred spinster would have looked demurely away before she noticed that...well... that an intimate part of him lay flaccid under the water.

She gulped, she blinked and she stared.

And what woman facing Rebecca's future would not? There might never be another opportunity for her to observe a man in all his glory. What a shame it would be to go her whole life and not know the way a man's hair grew beneath his clothing. How it dusted his thighs and curled on well-shaped calves, how it spread across his chest then narrowed to an arrow shooting straight at his—

What a wicked, wanton person she had become. Her father's child perhaps. Certainly her mother's.

The modest thing to do would be to tiptoe out of the kitchen, pretend that she had never come upon him. But Grandfather was counting upon his help with the cow.

Feeling flushed, she backed out of the room. From the parlor, she called his name softly.

No response.

"Lantree!" she shouted.

Silence, silence and more silence.

Very well, there was nothing left to do but shake him awake, to touch his naked shoulder with her bare fingers and jostle him until he opened his eyes.

The man was about to get the surprise of his life, but there was nothing she could do about that.

Rounding the kitchen door, she spotted a clean-looking dishcloth and snatched it up. She leaned over the tub and dropped it over his... A well-bred young lady should not even think the word.

With any luck, he wouldn't guess that she had glimpsed...well, to be honest, gawked at it.

By accident.

More or less.

Somehow she was going to have to erase that vision from her mind. If she didn't she would look guilty and he would know that she had only dropped the cloth after appraising his… Oh, by the saints!

She bent at the waist and shook his shoulder.

He smiled in his sleep but didn't wake up. She shook him again, harder this time.

"Lantree!"

He raised his hand to his shoulder and gave hers a squeeze. Was he, she could not help but wonder, dreaming of someone?

All of a sudden his other arm snaked around her waist and he toppled her down into the water. Her derriere hit smack on top of that little bitty dishcloth.

"Could be I was dreaming of you."

She certainly had not voiced that thought aloud…had she?

"You're awake!" Well, of course he was. What an idiotic thing to say.

"Have been since you set your boots to hammering my front door."

"You might have said something!" She scrambled to get out of the tub but only slipped about like a landed fish.

"I might have, but no matter if I spoke up or not, you were going to find me unfit company. I hoped you might go away."

"You might have warned me away."

He grinned. "If I had, I'd never know how pretty you look when you're flustered."

"Pretty! I will overlook the insult." Not that it would not still sting. "Because I did invade your bath."

"Why did you invade my bath?"

This time when she tried to get out of the tub he allowed it.

"There's trouble with Fancy's calf. Grandfather sent me to bring you to the barn."

All of a sudden the playfulness went out of his expression.

He rose from the water, holding the cloth in place.

She spun about and covered her eyes, even though the damage had long been done. "I'll meet you back in the barn."

"You'll wait for me." It sounded as if his voice was now coming from another room so she uncovered her face. "Your grandpappy would have my hide if I let you drown."

"In the rain? Really, I'm capable of surviving a raindrop."

He strode through the doorway from his bedroom, fully clothed with his hair slicked back and tied in a leather strap.

"Flash floods come up out of nowhere in these parts."

He grabbed her hand, held it tight in his big strong fingers until they reached the safety of the barn.

If there had been a flood lurking, conditions didn't show it. There had been only mud, water and more mud. But nothing of the magnitude of a flood.

When he stepped into the barn he let go of her, but not so fast that Grandfather did not notice and raise an eyebrow.

Lantree noted two things when he rushed into the barn.

Francie lying on the straw, and Hershal's smile when he saw him clutching Rebecca's hand.

Curse it! He'd been so caught up in the warm glide of her fingers against his that he'd neglected to let go before rushing inside.

For sure the old man would be up to some matchmaking now. Hershal had long insisted that he would be better off with a wife.

Seeing the cow lying still was a relief. It would be easier to deliver the calf when she was calm and not fighting against his help.

"Well now, Francie," he said, approaching her

with care. "Looks like you'll need some help this time."

He sat beside her, calming and reassuring her with a stroke on her nose.

"Can you bring the lanterns closer, Hershal? Our girl seems easy enough that she won't knock one over, but stay by just in case."

Thunder rolled over the roof. With the barn built as solidly as the house, and having no windows, the flash of lightning didn't intrude.

"I'll need your help, Rebecca."

Her expression was apprehensive, but her voice was not. "Tell me what to do."

"Strip down to your chemise."

"I beg your pardon?"

For someone who had recently ogled him in his bath, she appeared properly scandalized.

He stripped off his shirt, then pointed to a bucket of clean water.

"There's lye soap beside it. Wash up to your shoulders."

When she continued to stare dumbstruck at him he said, "It will reduce the risk of infection."

"I'll go fetch one of the hands," Grandfather said. "This is no business for a lady."

"Maybe not, but there's no time to go for help."

"Aunt Eunice did raise me to be a lady, Grandfather." Rebecca unbuttoned her wet shirt then peeled it off her shoulders and down her arms. "But not a helpless one."

She hurried to the bucket and thoroughly scrubbed her arms.

Lantree washed up after her.

If he warned her about what she might be called upon to do, he reckoned she would go screaming from the barn.

"Sit here beside Francie's head and talk gently to her, just don't touch her with your clean hands."

Delivering this calf was going to be difficult. He needed to turn it without Francie becoming panicked.

If she thrashed about, the results could be disastrous.

Luckily, Rebecca seemed to know what was required. Keeping her arms extended behind her she leaned down, close to the cow's ear. She spoke softly, or maybe she was singing.

He couldn't be sure of anything at the moment, because in leaning forward, the bodice of her chemise sagged. Right there in front of his eyes was the cleavage of a pair of fair-skinned, round and lovely breasts.

It was a lucky thing that Hershal, intent on guarding the lamps, did not notice where Lantree's attention had landed.

Even luckier, Rebecca, busy crooning to Francie, had not noticed.

The cow's belly suddenly hardened under his hand, drawing him back to the reason he was in the barn.

"I'm going to reach inside her as soon as this contraction quits, see if I can feel about for what's wrong."

Rebecca nodded. The color drained from her face. She laid her cheek on Francie's broad head.

"There will be a nice fat baby for you to love when this is over," she murmured.

Slowly he inserted his hand, then his arm up to his elbow, exploring gently.

He felt for a hoof and found it. Then he located another, and then a third. Two tiny hooves were already presenting, and there were three inside.

"Twins!" he announced. "Let's see if we can clear the way for the little fellows to come out."

Rebecca raised a brow but continued to whisper in Francie's ear.

"You'll need help," Hershal said, then he left the lanterns unattended and walked toward the bucket of water.

"Rebecca will have to do it, her arms are slender."

"That's no job for a—"

"Tell me what to do," Rebecca broke in then scooted toward him.

"Hold her tail up and away for now. I need to get this little fellow back inside."

The calf was nearly where it ought to be when he encountered resistance.

"Rebecca, let go of the tail. Run your hand alongside my arm."

He admired her. How could he not, when without hesitation, she reached inside a living, breathing cow.

"Do you feel a hoof? It's caught behind the pelvic bone. Belongs to the second calf. I think that's what's holding everything up." His breath came short, winded with the effort of holding the first calf in place while Rebecca located the oddly placed hoof.

"I feel it."

"Real gentle, now, push it backward. If you don't feel it returning to the same position, slowly withdraw your arm."

She nodded. Her head was close to his and he felt her damp hair brush his cheek.

"All right," she murmured. "It's out of the way."

When Rebecca's arm was free he said, "I'm going to do some positioning, then I'll need your help pulling this little guy out."

The turning proceeded better than he'd hoped it would, and when the hooves emerged again it was short work helping the calf into the world.

"Clear his nose. If he doesn't start to breathe tickle his nostrils with straw. If that doesn't work you'll need to breathe into his nose."

His attention was yanked from the newborn to the one coming all on its own. When this one was delivered he turned to see Rebecca mouth to nose with the firstborn.

What had been grudging admiration for Hershal's granddaughter had changed to full-blown respect, freely given.

By the saints, calves were sweet creatures. No wonder Fancy Francie licked them with such devotion.

In the hour after their birth, Barstow and the hands had visited, cooed over the newborns and declared them exceptional.

Indeed, they were perfect and beautiful in every way. One was a dark rich brown and the other reddish with white markings on its face and feet.

They all discussed names but in the end Lantree had suggested that Rebecca ought to do the honors since they owed their successful birth to her.

That was not true, of course. She had only done what Lantree had instructed her to.

Still, she did feel a glow having played a small role in the happy outcome. It tugged at a tender spot in her heart, watching the bond being forged between cow and calves.

She tried not to dwell on the fact that this kind of fulfillment would never be for her.

For now she would sit in the quiet barn and rejoice in this peaceful moment.

Earlier, when Barstow had gone back to the house, Grandfather went with him. Shortly after that, Jeeter yawned. Tom caught it and added a stretch. The pair of them returned to the bunk-house, grinning wide.

Even though it was late, she was not ready to retire to her room. She had told everyone that she would wait for a break in the rain, but really, she just wanted to sit in the dim light of the barn, breathing in the clean animal scents while listening to the storm blow across on the roof.

"I think I'll call the little bull Fancy Clancy, for his mama," she announced.

Lantree looked up from forking clean straw into Fancy's stall.

"It's a good name." He spread the straw over the dirt floor. "What about the little heifer?"

"Since she's the color of coffee, her name is Mocha...which I wish I had a cup of."

"You've earned it." He shot her a smile.

Well now, she'd help with calving every day in order to see his expression look so congenial.

He winked. Yes...yes he did, by George. He quite deliberately winked at her then walked into the tack room.

"What do you think of that, Miss Fancy? Or, I guess I ought to call you Mrs. given you are the mother of twins."

She stood up, walked toward Clancy then knelt beside him to give him a hug.

She had given this one his first breath. In her mind, they had bonded over it. Would he recognize that connection when he was grown and grazing free in the meadows?

The thought startled her. She hadn't even stopped to wonder if she would be here that long, she had just assumed that she would.

"This has got to mean that this is where I'm supposed to be, Clancy. I think I might be home...at last."

She stroked his ears. After a moment of admiring him, she walked over to the tall pile of fresh straw where Lantree intended to sleep tonight in order to keep an eye on Francie.

She sat down then flung herself backward, gazing up at the shadowed rafters with her arms spread wide.

It was late, after midnight. She ought to go back to the house. But the rain had grown heavier and the barn was cozy.

She closed her eyes. The straw felt plush between her shoulders. She wriggled into it, breathed deep and felt her lugs expand, her body go limp. She sighed, long and contented.

Then she smelled it…coffee!

Sitting up all of a sudden she saw Lantree standing ten feet away, a steaming cup in each of his big hands and an odd expression on his face.

"I didn't mean to rumple your bed," she said, embarrassed to be caught doing it.

"Stay where you are." His voice was gruff, but there was that smile again. She quite liked it.

She remained where she was but the lounging went out of her. She sat straight-backed, as prim and proper as the situation would allow.

Lantree settled beside her and handed her one of the mugs.

"Three cheers and an extra one for good measure." He tipped the lip of his mug against hers and let it linger for a moment.

"Thank you," she said and could not recall a time when she'd meant it more. The mug set in her fingers, warm liquid comfort.

"You earned it, that and more." He tapped the tip of his cup to hers. "On behalf of Francie and the calves, I thank you…we all do."

"I didn't do much, only what you told me to."

"Plenty of women would not have."

"You certainly seemed to know what you were doing." She took a sip of coffee even though it was steamy-hot.

"Most cowboys know what to do." He took a long swig from his mug and swallowed it slowly, looking hard at her while he did. "The truth is, I haven't always worked cattle. A lifetime ago I was a medical doctor."

What had happened? How could he say that and not expect her to be bursting with curiosity?

"Hershal hasn't told you anything about me, then?"

Her grandfather had told her plenty of things, all of them to convince her how wonderful Lantree was.

"He's never said anything about your past."

"I reckon you want to know."

Did she want to take her next breath?

"I wouldn't want to delve into personal matters."

"Everyone on the ranch knows my story. There's no reason you shouldn't."

He took another long draw on his coffee.

"Everything, I reckon, begins with Boone, my twin brother."

He was quiet for a moment so she said, "You have a twin? How very nice."

"It used to be, when we were kids."

"I never had a sibling. I wish I had." She did, however, have Melinda, and she counted her blessings every day for it.

Lantree drummed his fingers on his mug.

For someone who wanted to tell his story, he was slow to get to it.

"Believe me, you wouldn't want this one."

There was nothing she could say about that so she kept silent, waiting for him to continue.

"My brother made a mistake…a bad one. It ruined his life and shaped mine."

She bit her tongue not wanting to pry, but at the same time she desperately wanted to know what had made Lantree Walker who he was.

"When we were seventeen, Boone killed

a man. I don't think he meant to do it, but he was drunk and offended. The other man was even more drunk and offended than Boone was. My brother fired his gun without considering the consequences. I believe Boone was truly shocked to see the man clutch his chest and fall.

"I tried to keep the man from dying, but I was just a kid. I didn't know what to do. I just watched Boone run away scared, while the fellow he shot bled to death in my arms.

"I can't remember a time I ever felt so useless, guilty, too, since Boone was my twin. I decided that I would never sit by and watch someone die without knowing how to help. So I went to medical school believing that I could make a difference." He shrugged and took a long swallow of hot coffee.

"What happened to your brother? What became of him?"

"There was a witness. I didn't see him until after Boone had fled, but he stepped out of the shadows and told the marshal that my brother had fired in cold blood. I said he didn't, but a stranger's lie held more weight than a brother's truth. I reckon if Boone hadn't run it might have made a difference. But then, *might* is a damn shaky word. He could just as easily have been hanged outright. Plenty of things have been said about my brother over the years. To me they don't ring true to the boy I remember."

"Have you seen him since?"

He shook his head. The lantern's glow shimmered in his long hair.

"It must have been horrible for you…not knowing. I imagine it still is."

"In more ways than you can imagine. Especially once the wanted posters started circulating. I was arrested once and spent a week in jail before they figured out I wasn't Boone."

"I assume this is why you had to give up your career?"

He shook his head, then finished his coffee in one long gulp.

"It was something else."

She sensed that he was finished speaking about it. Unfortunately, she was not finished wanting to know more.

"Do you miss your old life…healing and saving lives?"

"A doctor's life isn't always saving lives. Sometimes, he's the only one left standing."

Outside, the wind raced around the eaves, making the sudden silence inside rife with the unspoken.

"There was a fever that came through my town. It killed a lot of people. I survived…but the doctor in me didn't."

"I'm so horribly sorry," she whispered through the tightening muscles of her throat.

He shrugged and shot her a quick smile. "Most days I'm content to be where I am. I love this wide-open country. If I had the choice of going back to the city or staying here…well, I reckon I'd stay here with your grandfather and the cows."

She could understand that. She felt the very same way. There was something about the land here, with its verdant valleys, its clear cold rivers and towering mountains, that captured you, made you know that this was home and nowhere else would do.

"Just so you know, Grandfather can't stop telling me how wonderful you are."

For an instant she thought… No, she didn't after all. Grown men did not flush when given a compliment.

"I didn't trust you in the beginning, I reckon you know that?" He shifted his gaze from her to the calves.

"I'm not convinced that you do now." There were moments like this one when he let down his guard in her presence, but other times he looked at her like he was sifting her soul for sins.

"I want to. I'd like nothing more than to believe that you have Hershal's best interests at heart."

"I love my grandfather." This conversation was taking a turn she was not comfortable with. "I can't imagine why you would believe that's not so."

She set her mug of coffee on the ground. All of a sudden it tasted bitter.

"I don't know you. Every day I watch Hershal growing more fond of you. At the same time, this ranch becomes more valuable. The timing of your arrival gets my curiosity going."

"You can put your suspicions to rest. I love my grandfather and would cut off my hands before I'd hurt him."

"So would I." He rested one elbow on his knee, then his chin on his open palm, which shifted his posture to lean closer to her. "Rebecca, I want to like you."

She matched his pose, tipping toward him.

"I want to like you, too."

She also wanted to slap him for thinking she would do her grandfather harm...but, and she could not deny this, she wondered what it would be like to kiss him.

It wouldn't take much to find out, just a slight forward movement and a pucker of lips.

"You are a beautiful woman, Rebecca."

Why, oh why, did he have to go and ruin a lovely moment?

She stood up quickly, the better to glare down at him.

Out of long habit, it flashed through her mind that maybe her father would have loved her enough to stay had she been more like Mama's pretty dolls.

Or perhaps not. Now that she knew something of the man, it might not have made a difference…but the plain truth remained: she did not have the kind of beauty to turn a man's head. The only person who thought so was Melinda and that was only because her cousin loved her.

"Just because you don't trust me does not mean you need to insult me."

"To be clear, Rebecca, that was a compliment, not an insult. Why do you get so fired up over being praised?"

Because…because… It hit her all of a sudden, a blow to the heart… She wanted him to think she was pretty…to really think it.

"I'm going back to the house."

"Wait while I get my coat."

"I'm capable of walking from here to the house on my own."

At the barn door, she felt the weight of his coat settle about her shoulders. It smelled like straw, coffee and newborn calves. She yanked the door open and the cool scent of wet trees and mud rushed inside.

From behind, his hands clamped down on her shoulders. His large, warm fingers turned her gently. It was impossible to deny the thrill that raced through her. She had to look up at him. It made her feel dainty, the way a woman ought to feel in a man's presence.

"I was not insulting you. You are beautiful."

"So are giraffes and elephants." Why could he not let her go peacefully on her way?

She didn't mind that she wasn't attractive. For an independent woman, strength of character was beauty.

He nodded. "Hippos and camels, as well. But Rebecca, none of them have lovely green eyes that make a man's heart skip over itself."

He touched her cheek, traced the arch of the bone under her eye then down to where it curved near her mouth.

With a gentle tug he drew his thumb over her bottom lip. How… What—

"Not a single one of them have lips that make a man forget caution all because he wants to kiss them."

"N-no," she stammered because her mind had turned mushy. "I do not suppose they—"

All at once he lowered his head and placed his lips where his thumb had been.

He smelled so… And his mouth felt so… And she was so…so hot. And confused, like her rational mind had fled and left behind a body that sparked everywhere Lantree touched her. Which was quite a few places since his hands were not idle.

It was good that her mind was not in control. She did not want it to be. What she wanted, wickedly wanted, was to feel his mouth where his big hands were kneading her breasts, making her nipples pucker to hard little nubs.

She leaned into his touch, and her breath hitched under his fingers. She only hoped that he did not notice how she was trembling.

How could her body feel as alive as the lightning striking outside while her mind was foggy? How was it that she wanted to strip off her clothes in order to be consumed by a man who "wanted to like her"?

In the next instant, there was cold space where his chest had warmed hers. He held her at arm's length, gripping her elbows.

She was out of breath and he could not seem to catch his.

"Never believe that you are not beautiful, Becca."

Drat the man! Of all the times to spout nonsense.

She yanked free of his hold, stomped out of the barn then slogged toward the house.

Behind her, his boots kept pace.

Remaining a dignified spinster had just become a whole lot more difficult, now that she'd had a taste of what could be between a man and a woman.

Chapter Eight

❦

Three days after the mistake in the barn, the storm finally moved on. Lantree got up before the sun because there were bound to be a dozen things that needed repairing.

Straightening two tipped fence posts and fixing a leak in the roof of the henhouse would keep him busy until Barstow had breakfast prepared. He'd gulp it down quick then ride out to see how the cattle had fared.

Normally, he wouldn't be grateful for the extra work that the storm had caused, but this morning he welcomed it like a stall welcomed a good sweeping.

Fresh air and extra chores might help purge the haunting going on in his mind…and his body. Maybe lathering up a hot sweat would make him forget how sweet it had been to hold

Rebecca in his arms, how her lips had been pliant and willing under his.

It might, but it probably wouldn't.

He shook his head and stepped onto his front porch. Predawn stars speckled the sky. The day would dawn bright with sunshine…a good day to work hard.

A lamp was already burning in the kitchen of the main house. Barstow must have gotten up early, knowing there was much to be done.

Since Lantree hadn't taken the time to light his stove to make coffee for himself, he was grateful that Barstow always brewed it first thing.

He'd grab a few swallows then head to the barn.

Entering the kitchen through the side door, he had a smile of appreciation ready for the cook.

Hellfire and brimstone! His grin landed smack on Rebecca as she sat at the table, her hair unbound and cascading over her shoulders in a silky fall.

He hadn't seen her since the incident. It had seemed prudent to keep to himself for a while, let things settle in his mind…let his body cool off.

Unfortunately, all the isolation had done was

increase those feelings and, no doubt, get everyone wondering what was going on with him.

When anyone questioned him he fired back with "Can't a man have a meal in his own house once in a moon?"

"It looks like it will be a lovely day," Rebecca said casually, as though she didn't recall how the earth had shifted when they'd kissed.

He had expected a frown of accusation from her, or a maidenly blush at the least.

But no. She simply smiled and offered to pour him a cup of coffee.

That just went to show how little he knew about her. It didn't seem likely, but maybe she was more experienced at kissing than he had first thought.

"No, thank you," he said about the coffee, even though he did want some. But not as much as he wanted to be on his way. "I thought Barstow was up, just wanted to say good morning to him."

"He was under the weather last night, so I told him to sleep in."

"What were his symptoms?" Hell, as soon as he kept to himself, someone got sick. "I'll see to him."

"He said to tell you not to bother him." Her

smile twinkled. If she had felt any angst over their intimacy it didn't show this morning. "It's just a sore throat."

"That's good. If it gets worse, send someone for me." He tipped his hat, forcing himself to remember that not every complaint turned into an epidemic. "I'll be on my way, then."

But…not before he set something straight. He paused with his hand on the doorknob. He turned around quickly enough to see that Rebecca's smile had sagged.

It was back in an instant though, which told him that it had not been a genuine smile at all.

For some reason that made him feel better… and worse.

Hell.

"Rebecca, I want to apologize for the other night. I was not a gentleman."

"No more than I was not a lady."

"You are every bit of a lady. I took advantage and for that I am sorry."

"You and I seem to have a long history of apologies between us, Lantree."

He walked back to the table but didn't sit down.

"Most of them from me," he admitted.

"The truth is, I lingered in the barn far past

the time it was proper to do so…and I think we were elated over Francie's babies."

"The time was ripe for…" The time was ripe for many things but none of them suitable. "Well, for friendship."

"It was, wasn't it? We both know where we stand on anything deeper than that, so…" She extended her hand. Her fingers were lovely, long and slender. "Let's shake on being friends."

That was fair, but what devil made him hold on to her a moment longer than he should have, long enough for Hershal to wander into the kitchen and see them touching.

"Lantree and I have decided to be friendlier to one another, Grandfather. Amicability is ever so much more pleasant than strife."

Hershal nodded, then turned in an attempt to hide his smile.

Lantree saw it but he didn't think that Rebecca had.

"I'll just take some coffee and get to work."

"Grandfather," he heard Rebecca say as he was going out the kitchen door. "I'd like to visit Grandmother's grave…and my father's."

Lantree froze midstep and stared at the skyline, which was still an hour from full daylight.

Hershal had not visited the gravesites, not

since the day he had shoveled dirt onto Catherine's coffin.

"Another time, perhaps," the old man answered. "The graveyard is a long way from here and it's rough going."

Lantree closed the door and walked toward the barn and his waiting chores.

Rebecca deserved to visit her father's and her grandmother's resting places, but he was certain that Hershal would never take her.

Maybe Lantree would, one day. One day when enough time had passed that he was not worried about being alone with her. When he was sure that it was friendship and friendship only between them.

It was understandable that Grandfather did not wish to visit the family plot. Some pain wrenched the heart so severely that all one could do was distance oneself.

Two days had passed since she had asked him to take her to the cemetery. He had not offered, so she would not ask again.

That did not mean that she was not going to go on her own. For all the men's talk about how dangerous the area was, she had only witnessed beauty.

This was her home now and she would not spend her life frightened of going beyond the yard. By the saints, the more familiar one was with one's environment, the safer one was in it.

Of course, if anyone knew she was venturing out, they would forbid it. Nonetheless, venturing out was what she was going to do.

It had been an easy thing to find out from Tom where the cemetery was located and an easier thing to get Jeeter to saddle her a horse for a ride around the paddock, or so he thought. He would discover her deception soon enough, but she would be long gone by then.

For now, here she was free and on her own, ready to enjoy the bright, warm day.

Her goal was simple. Ride to the cemetery, play a tune for Grandmother and one for Father, then be home before anyone missed her...or if they did miss her, before they could find her.

Life was grand in this bold, beautiful land. No one was going to keep her from enjoying it.

She rode the gently paced horse through green woods, over quiet streams and across meadows alive with yellow, orange and lavender flowers.

Cattle dotted the meadows, grazing serenely. If there was danger at hand, they would be the ones to know it.

Tom's description of the location of the cemetery had been accurate. She'd followed the sun west and come across the landmarks he had mentioned. At noon, according to the sun, she came upon a large boulder, at the foot of which was the cemetery.

A stone wall had been laid around the two graves lying side by side. She got off the horse then tied it to a tree a short distance from the burial plots.

Taking the violin from the saddle pack, she sat down upon the low wall, gazing at the names and dates carved into the rock.

"Thank you for the gift, Grandmother," she said.

She didn't mean the violin alone, but the love of creating music.

"Grandmother, did you feel it inside? Like you didn't even need sheet music to remember how to play a piece?"

Rebecca imagined that her Grandmother was sitting beside her, nodding.

Perhaps she ought to say something to her father…but what?

"I'm sorry your life went so wrong, Papa. I suppose you thought that leaving me and Mama was best for you back then. Well…I forgive you if that's any comfort."

Having said what she could, she lifted the violin from its case and began to play, something for Grandmother. Something lovely and inspiring.

Next she played something for her father, but it was melancholy, because the tunes she played tended to reflect what she was feeling at the moment. Perhaps with time she would play something lovely for Papa.

When she was finished, she set the violin back in its case and secured the clasps.

Wind rustled through the treetops. She closed her eyes and listened. She wanted to spend the rest of her life on the ranch, where even the elements made their own kind of music.

With the sun shining warm on her face she was convinced that the men of her new family had greatly exaggerated the danger.

Then she heard a noise that seemed out of place. She strained to listen.

"I'm telling you, I heard music," came a voice carried lightly by the breeze. The speaker was still hidden in the dense growth of trees.

She stood up suddenly because she recognized the voice. How long had it taken for Mike to spend all of her money? she wondered with a great deal of bitterness.

"You hear a heavenly choir to go with it?" another man declared, his tone mocking. "Come to think on it, we're near the Moreland graveyard…and you know what they say about Catherine Moreland."

Second by second the sound of feet tromping through the underbrush became louder. There would not be enough time to reach her horse.

"It's got to be her." The way Mike said "her," with a sneer, indicated that an encounter with the men would not be friendly.

The only thing to do was dash behind the boulder and hope that the men moved on.

"I say we cut some trees," the other man said, apparently ignoring Mike's mention of "her." "It's what we came for. Smothers won't be offering top dollar forever."

"The trouble with you is that you ain't got no vision."

From the sound of the voices they had to be near the stone wall. She pressed against the boulder, wishing that she had worn her brown dress instead of the bright yellow one.

"What I see is that this trip has been a waste of time. We haven't got a single tree into the river and floated it down to the mill. I regret that I ever came along."

"You won't regret it when you're a rich man."

"Wouldn't regret being handsome, neither, that don't mean it's going to happen."

"I've got a plan."

Rebecca had a sickening feeling that this plan involved her.

"What do you aim to do, Mike? Offer Smothers leaves instead of logs?"

"There you go again, no vision."

"What I see is lumber ready for the cutting."

"What about that horse over there? You see that?"

It had been a vain hope that they would not notice Clara munching the grass.

"What? By doggy, where'd that come from?"

"It was there to see the whole livelong time."

"I reckon we wouldn't get enough money for the nag to make it worth getting hanged as horse thieves."

"It's not the horse we're taking. It's the woman."

"What woman?"

"The one who was playing the violin, you half-brain!"

"I'd like to see you catch a ghost."

"I don't reckon ghosts ride mortal horses, do

you? It's Moreland's granddaughter we're going to take."

"You certain it was a mortal woman playing the music? Hope so, since old Moreland might pay good hard cash to get her back…sure more than he would a ghost."

"Not as much as Smothers will give us for her."

"Why would he give good money for Moreland's girl when he can have any whore cheap?"

"Think about it. He gets hold of her, marries her, then he's the one who inherits the ranch. He'll have all the trees he wants without having to pay a cent…and we don't have to work up a sweat cutting logs."

"The mayor is in a hurry. Could take some time for him to inherit."

"Could…or could not… Old men die all of a sudden and no one knows why."

Surely Mike was not talking about murder! But what else could he mean? Since he was clearly discussing kidnapping, why not killing, as well?

"Hey, girlie!" She hadn't noticed in their earlier encounter how evil Mike's voice sounded, but she did now and it made her stomach turn sour. "Come on out."

"We don't mean you any harm."

"You dimwit. If she's close enough to hear us and she likely is, she'll know that's not true." It sounded like Mike was at the wall now. "Let's make this easy, Miss Lane. Come along peaceful-like and we won't hurt you. Try and run... well now, that's a reason for punishment, and as I recall we have unfinished business of a personal kind between us as it is."

"Oooo-eee!" the other man yelped. "I hope she runs!"

Well, by the saints, she was not going to stay where she was.

The trouble was, if she ran, it would make noise. On the other hand, she didn't have time to move stealthily away from her pitiful hiding place.

The one and only thing she could think to do was to make them believe she had fled in another direction.

Thankfully, the wind came up and rattled the treetops, giving her cover noise to remove her shoes then pick up a rock.

When the blowing stopped, she hurled the rock away from her, then her shoes after it.

"That way!" the one called Dimwit shouted

and tramped toward the horse. "She's trying to get to her mount!"

Mike followed, hooting and shouting. She ran uphill, through the forest behind the cemetery, grateful that their noise covered the sound of her escape.

Without footwear she was at a disadvantage but wearing a yellow dress made her more so. She dashed between trees and had nearly reached the top of the rise when the men shouted.

They'd spotted her. How could they not, but instead of coming after her at a run, they took their time, whistling, hooting, calling her "girlie."

Clearly, they wanted to play cat and mouse. Let them. Many a mouse slipped to safety while the cat waited in vain.

While she was hardly mouse-like, she would think like one and find a place to hide.

She dashed off, hiding behind one wide tree and then another, all the while holding her skirt close to her body. She wasn't hidden from them but it was the most she could manage to do for now.

Since she was within their view, they would think they had her. Hopefully they would be so caught up in their fun that they would take their time.

That seemed to be true. The sound of the ruckus the men were making faded and seemed a bit farther away. She prayed that she was putting some distance between them.

When they tired of the antics, the situation would change. Two men in boots would cover the ground much more quickly than a woman in her bare feet.

Still, she did have the quicker mind. That and only that would be her salvation. If left to sheer strength the men would have her. Already she was winded, her feet sore and her side cramping.

Clutching her violin case close and glancing about, she spotted a trail of sorts, probably used by wildlife.

The path was not hidden. The men would spot her progress. But with any luck, that would keep them confident of catching her, keep them just a little bit slower than she was.

On the left side of the path there was the upslope of the hill. On the right the land sloped down, overgrown by thorny bushes.

The path itself was littered with leaves, which made the going easier on her feet, but the bushes snagged her dress and slowed her down.

Glancing back, she saw Mike charge ahead of Dimwit. As frightening as that was, it was also encouraging. He must now believe that she stood a chance of getting away.

That hope faded when she heard Mike's footfalls narrowing the distance.

She ran faster but something sharp sliced the heel of her right foot. She went down, heard Mike laugh. With a quick backward glance she saw him rushing toward her, a glint of victory in his grin.

Blood gushed from her foot but there was no time to do anything about that.

She stood, hobbling forward, but Mike was running fast…too fast.

Suddenly he was upon her, grabbing for her hair. She threw herself to the earth to keep him from snaring it.

That made him laugh, but from her position on the ground, she spotted something. To her right was a slide of sorts, made up of leaves that disappeared into the thorny growth. There was no telling where it led or how far, but at least it was away from Mike's grasping fists.

She launched belly-first. With her arms extended before her, and gripping her violin case, she closed her eyes. Branches ripped at her sleeves, then at her bare arms. She hit a large rock that knocked the wind out of her.

It seemed that she rolled, bumped and slid downhill for a very long time. Then, to her great shock, her face was suddenly underwater. She flailed about then sat up, chest deep in a cold stream.

As far as she could tell, she had left her pursuers behind, for the time being at least.

She stood, shaking with cold, fear and revulsion at the blood seeping from her many cuts and scrapes. But her foot was the worst of all. Pain throbbed to the beat of her heart.

She ripped a bit of lace from her petticoat and wrapped it, but still, she couldn't walk.

"Be the mouse…be the mouse," she muttered to keep from wailing in despair.

She might be free of her pursuers for the moment, but she had no belief that they had given up the hunt.

Beside the stream was a fallen log. She hopped on one foot toward it. All of sudden, she tumbled into a deep gouge in the earth. She hadn't seen it because it was filled up with leaves.

By the saints, if she curled her body into a tight ball, she might fit into it. She would need more leaves for cover, but the earth was littered with them, and a few dead branches, as well.

She crawled about on her knees, wincing when the scrapes gained from her tumble down the hill shot pain up her legs. Scooping the leaves into her skirt and even down her bodice, she collected enough to be able to hide herself. As hiding places went, it wasn't much, but she prayed it would be enough.

There was one more thing to do before she took shelter: get that miserable Mike off her trail.

She stripped off her dress, flinched when the fabric brushed the cuts on her chest and arms. And, oh, how she hated to do this, but she unwrapped her foot and squeezed the wound. She smeared the spurt of blood on the bodice.

She set the stained, shredded gown on a rock, letting the bottom half drag in the water. It wasn't likely, but she hoped they would think she had sustained a mortal wound and floated away downstream.

Good luck, little mouse, she thought as she crawled into the hole and buried herself in leaves and sticks.

"You reckon she drowned?" she heard Dimwit ask.

Rebecca's heart slammed against her ribs. Surely they must hear it thudding.

Mike's boot gouged the mud at the edge of

her hideout. One step backward and he would fall on top of her.

It was hard to tell how much time had passed since she had taken to her hideout. She guessed it ought to be near sundown, judging by the soft, dim light that filtered through the leaves.

"How's a dead woman going to get out of her dress then leave it on a rock?" Mike spat a glob of spittle on her leafy cover. "Naw, she lit out."

"Which way is what we better figure out. With all that blood she's trailing, the predators will take notice. Wouldn't care to lose our fortune to a bear."

"There's blood on this rock, here, but no place else. She must have stopped to wash," Mike pointed out.

"Or get washed away."

"Let's just figure that Lady Fortune is trying to get home. That means she's following the river north." That was something she didn't know. The fall had completely disoriented her. "Let's go that way for a few miles. If we don't get her we'll come back and head south."

Something tickled her nose… Something crawled across it! By closing one eye she could make out the fuzzy shape of a small creature with a lot of dark legs. She breathed, but shallowly. She squeezed her eyes shut, pretending to be anywhere else but in this hole with kidnappers above and creepy crawlers beneath.

"It's not like she'll get far with her foot cut up."

"She's real close by." Mike chortled. "I can feel that money bursting out of our pockets right now."

"We're as good as rich."

And she was as good as captured if the bug decided to explore her nostril.

Footsteps clomped noisily away. Three feet… seven it sounded now. Tiny bug feet tracked across the skin between her lip and her nose. *Fifteen feet… Please let them be…twenty feet away.*

The bug tested her nostril with a delicate scratch. She blew out the air in her lungs.

Praise the saints, the bug fell away from her nose. Mike's and Dimwit's footsteps faded into the forest.

She relaxed for the first time in…how many hours? It might not have been wise to do so but she closed her eyes, suddenly more weary than she had ever been.

It couldn't be long until they discovered that she had not followed the stream north. They would return.

So leaving the cold, damp hole was not an option. If she did she would leave an easy trail, for Mike and any other creature keen on the scent of blood.

Curled in a fetal position, her legs cramped, her hips ached and she twitched with the need to stretch out. And oh, her foot!

But whoever this Smothers person was—the mayor, Mike had said?—she was not going to marry him! Even more, she would not allow him to harm Grandfather. No matter how painful her joints became, she was not emerging, not for a very long time.

She forced herself to stay awake, knowing that the men would be returning. It would be a disaster to make some sort of noise or movement in her sleep to give her location away.

It was full dark before she heard them come back, cursing and at odds with each other.

They argued for a few moments. Dimwit wanted to stop the hunt, spend the night right here. Mike accurately pointed out that she could not have gotten far downstream, or anywhere else.

The discussion went on for a long time. They nearly came to blows, but they finally agreed to move on and return at daybreak if they didn't find her...or her remains, downstream.

With the deepening night came a chill. Being so close to the stream her dugout was damp.

Sleep, she had once heard, was the enemy when one was bone-deep cold. She tried to fight drowsiness, but she must have dozed, for she awoke with a start. Something smelly was snuffling at her leaf cover. It pawed and dislodged a stick.

When the leaves shifted, she saw the bulky shape of a huge bear. She felt the heat and heard the hiss of its breath when it sniffed her covering. No doubt the beast had been drawn by the scent of her blood.

Play dead. Hadn't she heard that somewhere, too? She lay very still and held her breath, even when a warm nose nudged her bare, lacerated shoulder.

After a long, terrifying moment, the bear moved on. She would not sleep again. No matter what, she would remain alert.

The trouble with remaining alert was that one heard every nocturnal sound. The pain of each cut and bruise was intensified.

And on top of everything, she did not have the luxury of crying over it.

But what she did have was her violin. She hugged it to her chest, grateful that in all that it had been through it had escaped with only a few scratches on the case.

The violin would save her tonight even if she could not take it out and draw the bow across the strings. What she would do was imagine the music in her head.

Fighting the urge to call up agitated notes, she let her mind summon something that reminded her of soft breezes and dragonflies floating on the warm air.

It worked for some time but then she began to hear something else.

Given the circumstances, the fear, the wounds and the shivering, she should not have been surprised to be having hallucinations.

By George, as delusions went, this one was quite pleasant.

"Rebecca!" Lantree's voice called softly.

A cold, gentle hand cleared away the leaves from her face, then swiped them from her body.

"What the hell, Becca?"

"You are very handsome," she whispered, because one could speak the truth to a vision and no one would be the wiser.

"And you are very battered."

Lantree's likeness slipped his arms beneath her and lifted her out of the hole.

She groaned because it hurt dreadfully. After being cramped for so long her joints and muscles screamed in objection to being freed.

This vision was quickly turning to a nightmare. She had to get back into her hiding place. She tried to crawl back to safety.

"Put me back," she pleaded and tried to scramble out of her vision's strong arms. "They'll be returning. How long is it until dawn, Lantree?"

"It doesn't matter, love. I've got you." He hugged her close to his big solid chest. "You're safe now."

"From Mike and Dimwit? From the bug and the bear?"

"From everything... I'm here, I've got you."

She sighed and snuggled close to her vision. "I've cut my foot. I'm trusting it to your care, handsome Dr. Walker."

Well then, it must be all right to sleep now. She closed her eyes and rested her head against his chest. For a figment of her imagination, he was exceptionally warm and solid.

Chapter Nine

Lantree sat beside Rebecca's bed, holding her injured foot in his lap and examining it while she slept.

Sleep was what they all needed right then. No one had gotten a wink of it since yesterday afternoon when they discovered that Rebecca was missing.

It had been an hour before dawn when he brought her home, then near dark when they finally pieced together what had happened. That had been twelve hours with everyone worried to the bone.

The bald truth was that she had behaved in a foolhardy manner, but he could not fault her for wanting to visit the family resting place.

He should have volunteered to take her. The blame for her condition lay partly on him.

It would be a long time before he forgot how

he'd found her…shivering, bloody and wedged into that muddy hole in the ground. If it hadn't been for a sideways glance, he would never have noticed the yellow dress strewn over the rock beside the stream. He would have passed by, leaving her to die of exposure more likely than not.

As it was, she had been delirious for the better part of an hour on the ride home. He'd wrapped her up in the blanket he kept on his saddle and held her in front of him, stoking her arms and her back to warm her.

The situation had been dire, but now that she was safe in bed, cleaned up and dozing soundly, he couldn't help but smile.

Rebecca Lane, in her delirium, had been complimentary…of him in particular.

He'd discovered that she especially liked his hands because, and she had declared this with certainty, they were big and bold, but also gentle…and very warm. His former fiancée, being a petite woman and delicate to her core, had always been apprehensive about his hands. He'd never given her reason to be but now, thinking back, she'd been apprehensive about many things.

Another thing he had discovered was that Rebecca liked being able to look up at him…he was, again in her words, "A gigantic and pleasing example of manhood."

No doubt if he teased her about it now, she would deny everything that she had said. She would because she would not remember it.

She had also been confident in his ability to care for her injuries. Her trust had ignited something inside of him. Given him a glimmer of confidence he thought had died.

"What do you think?" Hershal asked from where he had been sitting silent vigil in a chair on the other side of the bed.

Drawn back to the task at hand, he studied Rebecca's long, shapely foot.

"The cut is deep," he admitted. "I'll need to make some sutures."

"Will the pain wake her up?"

"I reckon we'll see." He reached for the clean needle.

He took the first stitch. The process came back to him as though he had done it only yesterday.

"I take to heart every word of the story she told us." Hershal shook his head, his gray brows narrowed to an exclamation point. His anger was obvious. "I'd hang those low-down guttersnipes from the barn rafters by their feet if I could get away with it."

"I believe her, too. If Mike and that other fellow are lurking about, Jeeter will find them. It goes against the grain but we'll have to settle for handing them over to Johnson. But I reckon they'd rather face a barn rafter than Liver-Eater's enforcement of the law."

Rebecca moaned in her sleep when he applied the next stitch.

"If she comes to it will hurt a whole lot more."

"It's not even my foot and I'm feeling green." Hershal rose from his chair, looking stiff from sitting so long. "I'll see you at supper."

"I'll be along when I can," he answered without looking up from his task.

As soon as the door closed, Rebecca let out her breath in a rush.

"By George, this isn't as horrible as I feared it would be."

She bit her bottom lip. It was probably worse than she thought it would be.

"How long have you been awake?"

"Since you poked a needle and thread into my foot."

"Sterilized catgut…and I'm sorry but it's got to be done."

She nodded, inhaling a shaky breath. "Let's get on then, Doctor. Dawdling will only prolong it."

There was no denying that he liked hearing the title she had given him. It had been some time since it had felt good.

"Only three more to go."

"Remind me to post a notice around my neck," she said through gritted teeth.

He felt bad about the pain he was inflicting on her. No doubt, talking was her way of getting through this.

"It will say in bold letters, 'Rebecca Lane will not be forced into marriage.'"

"That's fair." He carried on the conversation in order to distract her from the next stab of the needle. "You can count on me to defend your right to remain an independent woman."

"Thank you. If my aunt could not bind me to the butcher, that blasted thief Mike will not tie me to...to the mayor...of Coulson, was it?"

"Smothers. Don't worry about him... There now, all finished." He patted her ankle. "You were a model patient."

"Thank you, Lantree." She brushed a strand of hair away from her temple with the back of her hand. "Not only for mending all my cuts and scrapes, but for going out into the night to look for me. You are…well… What you are is my hero."

There wasn't much to say to that. It felt damn good to be a pretty lady's hero.

"Get some rest. I'll have Barstow bring you up some supper later."

"That won't do. I'll come downstairs to eat."

"The men will be relieved to see you." How could he not admire Rebecca Lane? Eloise would have lain abed for a week soaking up the attention. "I'll be back to help you down the stairs."

"I'm sure I can manage it on my own. After all I—"

"Have fresh sutures in your foot. I'll be back."

He shot her a frown then closed the door to further argument.

For some reason, his step felt lighter on the stair, and he was smiling.

Rebecca relaxed in her chair before the hearth. The night was cool but only required a small fire.

To her right sat Grandfather and Barstow. On her left were Lantree, Jeeter and Tom. The line of chairs formed a semicircle about the fireplace to make conversation easier.

She loved this time of evening, with the work of the day finished and everyone safe at home. It was especially nice now that Lantree had taken his usual place once again.

As usual, Kiwi Clyde joined them for the evening gathering.

The bird sat on the back of her chair, gently nibbling her hair and making kissing noises.

One might believe he had the disposition of a lamb.

"I reckon he's not so bad," Lantree said, reaching a finger toward the bird, possibly meaning to stroke his feathers.

"He's a bird in a million." Barstow nodded his head vigorously.

"I love you," Kiwi Clyde said quite clearly then scooted toward Lantree.

The bird continued to make friendly kissing sounds. Lantree stroked his chest with the back of one finger.

Without warning, without an apparent change of mood, Kiwi Clyde bit down hard on Lantree's finger. A pearl of blood welled from his skin.

"Good boy!" the bird declared.

"I saw that one coming." Grandfather chuckled.

"You might have said something!" Lantree

wrapped his finger in a kerchief that he drew from his pocket.

When the laughter settled, Grandfather cleared his throat.

"As a matter of fact, I do have something to say." Grandfather stood up as though he were about to make a speech, or at least a proclamation.

He stood tall, drew his shoulders back. He was the owner of this spread, the man in charge, and his authority showed.

"It's become clear to me, and I'm certain to you all, that our Becca is no longer safe."

Certainly that was an exaggeration. Had she not just proved that in a desperate situation she could defend herself? It was true that she needed help getting home, but she had been the one to evade her pursuers. They were men who were at home in the mountains, and she had bested them.

Back in Kansas City she had managed to keep herself safe and she could very well do it here.

Grandfather would be made aware of that as soon as he finished pointing out her vulnerability.

"Therefore, I have decided that my granddaughter and Lantree will marry."

She leaped to her feet and winced at the pain slicing through her foot.

Lantree frowned, cursed, then scooped her into his arms as though she weighed no more than a mite.

Grandfather grinned, looking thoroughly pleased with himself.

"Keep off that foot," Lantree hissed, then set her back down in the chair. He handled her gently even though his expression was thunderous. "Have you lost your mind, Hershal?"

"He has, by George! He's become addled." Normally, she would not say such a thing, but very clearly Grandfather's mind had become suddenly muddled.

Tom leaped from his chair to pound Lantree on the back. "Congratulations, Doc!"

Lantree glared at him.

"We need some whiskey for a toast!" Jeeter exclaimed, his face beaming in anticipation.

"I'll fetch a bottle of wine." Barstow grinned and clapped his hands. "You, young man, will be given one sip."

"But this is a big event," the boy complained.

"It's not an event at all!" Rebecca glanced up at Lantree, who stared back at her, clearly stunned.

Barstow returned with the bottle of wine. He, Jeeter, Tom and Grandfather tipped their glasses…three times.

She set hers on the hearth beside Lantree's.

"You can't just decree something like that, Hershal," Lantree argued. "You know I have nothing to offer a wife."

"You have safety to offer her."

"That ought to keep a roof over her head."

"This will be the roof over her head." Grandfather certainly did appear pleased with himself and his half-brained plan. "As soon as the pair of you are married, I'm handing this ranch over to the both of you…joint owners."

"Well, damn it, Hershal, that's half-cocked thinking!"

"You owe me, boy. I saved your hide once, now you will save my Becca's life."

"My life is not in danger, Grandfather, and even if it were, I am perfectly capable of defending myself."

A long silence, frowns and shaking heads answered her.

What was wrong with the male race, thinking they were the salvation of anyone having breasts?

"I will not be forced into marrying anyone."

She crossed her arms over the evidence of her feminine inferiority. She was angry, so much so that she felt her heart beating against her arm.

"And I stand by her right to make that decision," Lantree said.

By the saints! From out of nowhere his statement touched her, made her feel... Oh, how she didn't want to admit this, but it made her feel safe...protected.

"Lantree and I agree. We will not marry."

"The sooner the better, is all I have to say on the matter." Barstow lifted Kiwi Clyde off the back of the chair.

"We'll make the announcement in Coulson. Be ready to travel day after tomorrow, early." With that, Grandfather hugged her then shook Lantree's hand. "I know you'll take good care of my girl."

He looked so proud, as though she and Lantree had just professed undying love and could not wait to recite their vows. Aunt Eunice was a novice at manipulation compared to Grandfather. Who would have guessed that a sweet-looking old man could wield such power, or at least believe that he did?

"I can't leave my work here," Lantree pointed out to Grandfather's retreating back.

"That's an insult to Jeeter and Tom. This won't be the first time they've stepped in for you."

Without further comment, Grandfather disappeared up the stairwell.

"Looks like I've got some food to pack up for the trail." Barstow walked toward the kitchen on his small feet, making the floorboards creak.

"Sweet dreams, lovebirds," Jeeter called, going out the front door with Tom.

She was left alone gawking, probably very unattractively, at Lantree.

"We most certainly are not lovebirds." She looked to Lantree for confirmation.

"And we are not in any way engaged."

But what they were, and what they had never quite been before, was allies.

As she did each afternoon, Rebecca visited Francie and the calves. They had been released from the barn and allowed to roam the paddock.

The south corner of the paddock was shaded by a stand of huge leafy trees. On this hot day, the cows sought shelter under them.

"Hello, my pretty girls, and my handsome boy," she said, stroking each bovine ear.

She sat down on a stump, enjoying the shade and the rustle of the leaves high above her.

Lantree strode out of the barn. He tugged his hat low over his forehead to ward off the sun. As soon as he spotted her, he waved. His boots crunched the dirt and his leather chaps chaffed against each other as he crossed the paddock.

Watching him, she did have to admit that if a woman were to marry, this man would be— No, never mind that. He was not right for her in any way, except for his height and his big gentle hands and his sultry blue eyes that observed the world from under lowered brows much of the time.

If only Melinda were here. He would be just the man for her pretty cousin.

Watching the play of sunlight and shadow cascading over him as he crossed the yard, she remembered when she and her cousin were young, their hearts just beginning to flutter at the idea of falling in love with a man.

In bed late at night, they would talk about what the man who would sweep them away would be like. Blamed if they hadn't concocted a hero just like Lantree Walker, from his long windblown hair to his confident stride.

Over the years, while Melinda had grown to

be a beauty, Rebecca had grown tall, lanky and plain. Not at all the type of woman to turn a man's head, especially a man like Lantree.

Watching him wipe the sweat from his brow with his shirtsleeve, she decided that the same could not be said of Melinda. She could turn any man's head. And Lantree would be her dream come true.

"The calves are growing fast," he commented, but she knew that was only polite conversation and not what was really on his mind.

They had not spoken since last night when Grandfather had proclaimed them engaged. She had some things to say to him and she supposed he felt the same way.

"Do you have a moment?"

He nodded then sat down on the stump beside hers.

"I was awake all night, thinking." She clenched her hands in her lap, nervous about telling him what conclusion she had come to.

"So was I."

"I know, I saw your lamp go off half an hour before sunrise."

He loosened the kerchief around his neck then undid the first two buttons of his shirt.

"It's a blister today. If you want to loosen your collar I'll consider you sensible and not brazen."

"Not long ago you'd have offered me a dollar." She couldn't help but laugh, remembering the misunderstanding between them in the beginning.

"And you'd have stitched my mouth closed for making the suggestion."

He laughed along with her. How very nice. She hadn't had this easy rapport with anyone since she'd said goodbye to Melinda. Not even with Grandfather, as much as she loved him.

While she would prefer to sit all afternoon enjoying the way his smile crinkled the corners of his eyes, now was the time for a serious discussion.

"It's true what your grandfather said." Lantree spoke up before she had a chance to. "I do owe him."

"I think we ought to consider what he had to say… Not that we should marry, of course, only that we ought to understand his reasoning."

"You may not like this any more than I do, but as far as reasoning goes, his is sound." Lantree shrugged his shoulders. "Let's just say that we did what he wants. It would protect you from anyone trying to get at the ranch through you."

He was right, marriage would make her unapproachable.

"My protection is what Grandfather has in mind, I know, but it's his safety that worries me." A chill prickled the skin on the back of her neck, remembering what Mike and Dimwit had suggested about the length of her grandfather's life.

"We are in a hard place, and no way about it. Becca, it's hard to ignore the fact marrying would resolve the problem."

Drat, why did her heart have to flutter when he used that endearment? And why had he used it, since their relationship was nothing more than companionable…and that only recently?

"What if we go along with Grandfather's scheme?" She took a deep, steadying breath, hesitant to divulge the conclusion she had come to in the wee hours of the night. "To a point, that is. Let him announce our engagement and then make it a very long one. We could pretend to be engaged. It might give us the same results as actually tying the knot."

He nodded. "It might, but it would take some playacting on our part to make it believable, at least when we are in Coulson. Is this something you are agreeable to?"

"I'd do anything to protect my grandfather."

He nodded. "Good, so would I."

"Well, then." She extended her hand. "Do we have an agreement?"

He grinned. The heat of his smile did things to her insides…fluttery, coiling things that a woman like her was better off not knowing anything about.

His big hot hand closed about hers, swallowed it up, in fact.

"Here's to keeping loved ones safe," he declared.

Chapter Ten

Lantree called a halt to travel late in the afternoon, deciding that they would spend the night in a shady glen where he and Hershal had camped many times in the past.

The area was protected on the north by a rock wall. A waterfall spilled over it and created a sparkling pond. For the most part, it was a convenient and secure refuge. The flower-studded meadow made it one of the prettiest places he knew of.

If all went well, they would arrive in Coulson tomorrow, midday, make the fake announcement then head home.

By the looks of Rebecca, a night in the hotel couldn't come soon enough. Not that she had complained. He had learned that she was not one to do so.

Here was a woman who met life's obstacles

with her chin held high, and usually with a smile on her face. She did not shy from adversity but met it eye to eye.

It would be fair to say she was not like any woman he had ever met. Certainly not the conniving female he had, at first, thought her to be.

Although she would not admit to being tired, it was evident in the slight droop of her shoulders, and the hitch in her breath when she wiped the sheen of perspiration from her brow.

Given a choice, he would not have picked the hot weather to travel in, but the sooner they announced this sham engagement, the safer Hershal and Rebecca would be.

While Lantree watered the team and set them to pasture, Hershal found a shady tree, spread his bedroll and fell deeply into a nap. The rumble of his even snoring drifted over the campsite.

Rebecca returned from a trip to the pond carrying a bucket of water. Her foot must hurt like the dickens but she didn't let it show.

"I'm going to gather firewood," he told her. "If there's any trouble, wake your grandfather and have him fire his gun. I'll be back on the run."

"I'm sure we'll be fine."

Rebecca lifted her hair with one hand and

fanned her bare, sweat-dampened neck with the other.

Even though he, too, was nearly sure there would be no trouble, he would make quick work of gathering the wood.

Within fifteen minutes he had picked up what he could carry or drag. He returned to the campsite, dropped the load then nearly tripped over it.

Not fifty feet away, a sea nymph was rising from the pond.

Stunned to silence, he could only stare while water sluiced off her naked body. Glistening rivulets slid down her shoulders then around high, firm breasts. Droplets fell from the pink tips. Watery fingers caressed the dip of her trim waist, pooled in her navel then rushed to tickle the dark hair at the apex of her long, lovely thighs.

While it seemed that time had suspended, that he'd stood there gawking at her for a long time, the truth was he'd spotted her then instantly turned away.

For all his staring at the treetops, the pile of wood and a beetle crawling across the dirt, the sight of his false fiancée remained sizzling on his eyeballs.

He'd seen portions of her body in a professional way when he'd cleaned up her scrapes, but hell and damn, watching Venus rise from the water gave him another reaction entirely.

Since she seemed oblivious to him while she enjoyed the cool relief of the pond, he returned to the forest to gather another load of wood.

By the time he returned, she was dressed and sitting on a log, squeezing the water from her tangled hair with long, shapely fingers.

From now until whenever they parted company, it would be impossible to look at her in the same way again.

What the hell had happened in her past to make her believe that she was homely, fit only for spinsterhood?

If things were different, he'd consider making Hershal a happy man. If he would make a fit husband for anyone, he would court Rebecca Lane, properly and with marriage in mind.

"You look—" *damp and seductive, provocative, tempting* "—refreshed."

"For a while, at least." She flashed him a smile and flicked water from the ends of her hair. "I'll be glad when this heat spell ends."

"It ought to pass in a day or two."

It ought to, if one was speaking strictly of the weather. He reckoned the red flush inside him would linger for a good long time.

* * *

Rebecca might have felt threatened coming into Coulson but, somehow, she didn't. While there was every chance that Mike and Dimwit were in town, with Lantree sitting on the wagon bench to her right and Grandfather to her left, the both of them well armed, she felt secure.

It also helped that the town did not seem as wicked to her as it had the first time she had seen it.

Today there were ranchers walking the streets. They appeared to be conducting legitimate business.

She didn't spot any wives, but perhaps they were secured away in the one hotel that did not double as a brothel.

A man, well dressed and pot-bellied, was standing on the porch of the trading post, clutching the lapels of his coat while giving some sort of impassioned speech. Farmers and saloon patrons cheered, then booed, and then cheered again. The speaker seemed to lead their reactions much like a conductor leads his orchestra. Up and down the voice of the crowd went according to his direction.

As they rolled closer she could hear the man's preaching clearly. Unless something was done to prevent it, he admonished, his fist now clenched and pumping the air, Coulson would die and Billings would thrive.

To her way of thinking, if Coulson died it would be because Billings was a better town.

She looked with interest at the lawman standing behind and to the right of the speaker. His matted hair stood on end, and his long beard brushed the shotgun that he clutched across his chest.

All of a sudden she felt Lantree stiffen. Grandfather cursed, his bony hand fisted into a ball.

"He's noticed her," Lantree said.

She shifted her gaze to find the speech giver staring directly at her while the crowed cheered his remark about Coulson becoming a great hub of commerce.

"I was hoping to announce the engagement before Mike told him about our girl." Grandfather curled his arm about her shoulder and squeezed.

"He's Smothers?" It made her stomach turn to think that if it hadn't been for a convenient hole in the ground she might, at this moment, be that man's very miserable bride.

"You have nothing to fear from him." Grandfather patted her shoulder. "He's got a big mouth and loves power, but when it comes down to it, I reckon he's yellow to the bone. He won't try anything, not with your big, strapping fiancé to protect you."

Grandfather and Lantree exchanged a quick glance that they probably didn't want her to notice. Perhaps this Smothers was more dangerous than her protectors were letting on.

"That's right. Our engagement will keep you safe." He grinned at her and winked, a silent acknowledgment of their private agreement.

Lantree clicked to the team and steered them toward the general store.

While her big strapping "intended" went inside to purchase some things for Barstow, Grandfather took her for a walk.

He introduced her to the folks they passed on the boardwalk. She was surprised that nearly everyone knew him.

"Doc Brody, I'd like to introduce my granddaughter, Rebecca Lane," he said to a saloonkeeper who had come out of his establishment to breathe some fresh air. "She and my foreman, you recall Lantree, are engaged. We've come to town to spread the good news."

"You have my best wishes, Miss Lane." The saloon owner appeared pleased with the announcement. "Walker is a good man. I've reason to know that."

By George, she'd never met a saloon-keeper before. He didn't seem to be a wicked person. There would be the devil to pay, though, if Aunt Eunice ever discovered that she had shaken his hand and accepted his good wishes.

But Aunt Eunice would not find out. A sense of lightness, an awareness of new freedom, made her smile from her heart. If Rebecca turned cartwheels in the street…barefoot…her aunt would never know.

It wasn't as if Grandfather did not put restrictions on her behavior, but those were simply a matter of her safety. As far as social behavior went, she was free to shake Doc Brody's hand.

Grandfather and Doc Brody spoke for a few moments about the arrival of the railroad in August.

When the men finished their conversation, she and Grandfather walked on, speaking with this farmer and that drunk. Once he even introduced her to a woman named Sweetbriar who wore rouge on her lips.

"I know that your aunt raised you with high standards, Rebecca, and I hope you aren't offended by the folks I'm introducing you to, but the more people who know about your engagement, the less chance there is of Smothers getting away with anything."

"What Aunt Eunice does not know will not shame her."

After an hour of strolling with Grandfather she discovered that there was something that respectable folks and not-so-respectable folks had in common.

One and all, they were excited about the arrival of the railroad. The thrill of what was coming fairly buzzed in the air. Prosperity was on the way...the threat of Billings notwithstanding.

As they walked, passing the trading post, a saloon and then the bank, she said, "Coulson isn't quite as wicked as I first thought."

"It's early, Rebecca. Come sundown, people will get drunk and mean. Even some of the ones that you met who seemed polite as pie."

Approaching the sheriff's office, she spotted the lawman studying the wanted posters tacked to the outside wall.

"He seems an odd one," she muttered.

Grandfather blew out a breath. "Liver-Eating Johnson is not a man to cross."

With a grunt and a shake of his head, Johnson went back inside his office.

If the broadsheets were anything to go by, there were certainly a lot of wanted men…and even one woman. Some of the posts looked old and crinkled, others new and bright.

In Kansas City, she had never even seen a—

All at once, she gasped. She dashed toward the wall and snatched a broadsheet off its nail. She prayed that Johnson had not seen her do it. This had to be an illegal act.

Well, by the saints, she did not care.

"Moreland!" a voice shouted.

The mayor strode toward them, his well-fed belly leading the way. She dashed the paper behind her back, wadded it into a ball.

"Stand behind me, Rebecca," Grandfather ordered, as if by doing so she would be hidden from Smothers's sight.

She felt silly ducking behind him, but Grandfather had his pride and she would not injure it. That didn't mean her mind was not at work figuring a way to best avoid the portly mayor in the event he made a move to snatch her. She ought to have brought Screech along. The bird was protective and he had a mean beak.

"Did your man deliver my message?" Evidently Smothers was not big on social talk. He went straight to the heart of the matter. "I need trees…I'll pay fair price."

"Get your trees from somewhere else. Mine aren't for sale."

"The future of this town is at stake. It's your civic duty to hand them over."

"My duty is to protect my granddaughter. Just so you understand, I'll skin you if you look sideways at her. Mike might have given you some ideas in regards to her, but you'd best forget all about them. Let's go, Rebecca. Your intended is waiting for us at the hotel." Grandfather took her arm and turned her away, but not before she noticed that the mayor's face was turning red… nearly purple to be accurate.

"Intended? My congratulations to the bride." Smothers's lip lifted at one corner in an unattractive sneer. "I wish you…luck."

That was as bald a threat as she'd ever heard. It didn't set well to let it go without a response but Grandfather was hustling her away so quickly that all she had time to do was toss back a glare.

Hershal had done his part by escorting Rebecca about town and announcing the engagement. Now it was time for Lantree to play his role.

"You ready for this?" he asked Rebecca.

She slipped her arm through his and nodded.

They stood on the front porch of the new hotel. It hadn't been here last time he was in town. Evidently the place had been tacked together in a hurry in anticipation of the newcomers who would be arriving by train in August.

"I don't think it's the best idea to be out in the open," she whispered.

"I understand this is uncomfortable for you, but I can't think of another way to make sure folks believe we are in love, ready to make the big leap."

"It's not that, Lantree, I need to tell you what—"

From the corner of his eye, he spotted Smothers coming out of the barbershop across the street. There was nothing to be done but cut straight to the matter at hand.

He kissed Rebecca Lane. She had been in the middle of speaking but he cut her off. Let her protest later if she wanted to.

Her lips lay under his, tense and unresponsive. He couldn't say why he was disappointed. This was all for show and they both knew it. Maybe he had hoped to taste more of the fire that he had sampled in the barn. He had reason to know that there was a great deal of passion inside this self-appointed old maid. Some devil inside urged him to put kindling to her flame.

Deepening the kiss, he drew her in, closer to his heart.

Next, he brushed her ear with his lips, as though he were whispering endearments.

"Sorry...didn't mean to pounce, but Smothers is across the street," he murmured and caught a whiff of her scent, the very scent that had intrigued him from the very first day.

He felt her sudden intake of breath. She leaned into him then looped her arms about his neck.

"He frightens me and I don't mind admitting it...but what I was trying to tell you—" She gazed up at him, so pretty and sincere. Her lips pouted as though she wanted another kiss. Anyone watching would believe it. By hell, he nearly believed it. "—was that I found this."

"I love you, too, Muffin," he declared loud enough for a man weaving down the boardwalk to overhear.

"Not as much as I love you, Tadpole."

Tadpole? She reached into her pocket then pressed a wad of paper into his hand. It felt suspiciously like a broadsheet.

Smothers walked one door down then entered

the Scarlet Dove Saloon. There was no missing his parting glare before he closed the big red door behind him.

The man might be the mayor, but there was nothing of the upstanding citizen about him. He was as crooked as most everyone else in Coulson.

"Don't be frightened…I'm here, Becca."

She lifted up on her toes and kissed his cheek. Even though the affectionate gesture was not genuine, it sent a thrill racing through his blood.

"Let's skip the rest of our walk," she whispered, her breath beating warm against his ear. "You need to see what I just handed you. Besides, Grandfather is waiting for us in the dining room."

He nibbled her lips, whispering between pecks, "I've seen the like before. You need a ring."

"But you—"

"I'm relieved to know that my brother has not been hanged yet."

He kissed her again but she did not respond to the coaxing of his mouth, not even with a sigh. In the end, as much as he'd like to get a reaction from her, it was best that he hadn't.

For both of their sakes, it might be best to leave some fires unstirred.

He led her across the street with his arm about her shoulder, demonstrating to anyone who was watching, and many people were, that she was his.

At the trading post, he bought her a set of glimmering gold rings. He slipped the engagement ring onto her finger then tucked the wedding band into his pocket.

No one was looking at them, but her eyes widened anyway. When she glanced up at him with a smile, it did something to his heart.

Twenty minutes later, he and Rebecca sat at a table in the hotel dining room sharing a bottle of wine with Hershal.

As much as he didn't want to dwell on the poster that Rebecca had snatched from the sheriff's door, he wondered how many people had seen it. Perhaps he ought to make some kind of public announcement that he was not Boone Walker.

But hell and damn, he'd tried that once before and still spent a week in jail. He couldn't afford to be locked up for even a day, not with having to watch out for Rebecca.

Tonight his boss was full of satisfaction, believing that his harebrained scheme was working.

So far, nothing had happened to indicate that it wasn't.

But there was a feeling in Lantree's bones that trouble was coming.

Could be that the uneasiness was due to seeing Boone's image and the dollar amount that his brother's life was going for. Or it could be something more imminent.

Either way, it would be a long, restless night.

Rebecca sat on her bed and gazed about the hotel room. It was small but clean. The paint still smelled fresh. If one did not hear the debauched heartbeat of Coulson's nightlife pulsing through the thin walls, one would be able to sleep.

If she could close her eyes without reliving Lantree's kiss she might be able to doze. She sighed, suspecting that the memory of that hot, earth-tipping moment might keep her awake forever.

It had taken her entire power of will not to melt and moan against him. It would have been so easy to forget they were actors in a skit.

Even if circumstances were not what they were, a man like Lantree, so big and well muscled, so very virile, would not be attracted to a big, plain-looking woman. The sooner she laid to rest the forbidden feelings that he had stirred up inside her, the better off she would be.

Perhaps the fact that these feelings were forbidden was what made them so intense. That was something to consider.

Drumming her fingers on the coverlet, she continued to glance about the room, looking for some distraction.

Maybe she ought to recite her well-practiced reasons why remaining a spinster was for the best.

One, no man would tell her what to do… Two… Blame it, the reasons were beginning to fade. However, the part about no man ever telling her that he loved her was thundering in her mind.

By the saints! She looked high and low for something of interest to douse that thought.

Lantree had warned her not to open the window. Grandfather had threatened dire consequences if she did.

But it was near midnight and the room still held the heat of the day. The temperature outside had to be cooler than it was inside.

She could scarcely breathe the heavy air. Her

shift was drenched in sweat. It stuck to her skin, hot and clammy.

If she disobeyed and opened her window, Grandfather had guaranteed that a reprobate would climb through it. But if she did not open her window she would suffocate.

She got out of bed and slid the window up a few inches.

In the unlikely event that an intruder tried to creep through the crack, she would make sure to be prepared.

She glanced about the dim space. There was a brass candlestick on the writing desk. Beside the desk was a wooden chair. She would make simple work of the miscreant by knocking him over with the chair then rendering him unconscious with the candlestick.

This was an excellent plan for two reasons. The first was that an unconscious intruder would be unable to assault her. And the second was that it would prove to Grandfather and Lantree that she was well able to take care of herself under any circumstance.

When she thought about it, she would be doing Lantree a favor. Now, with Boone's likeness having been on public view for who knew how long, he was going to have to leave the ranch and look for a safer place to live. But where could that possibly be? If Montana was not safe enough, where would be?

By George, she really was doing him a favor. When he discovered how well she was able to take care of herself and Grandfather, he would be able to ride off with a clear conscience.

She plucked the candlestick from the table then scooted the chair across the floor and set it beside the bed.

She was right about the air being cooler outside. A blessed draft blew in through the crack. She fanned the neckline of her shift against her skin and then climbed back into bed. Sitting up, she rested her head against the headboard.

By the saints, her eyelids were heavy. What could it hurt to close them, as long as she kept her ears open in the odd chance that Grandfather was right?

Grandfather was right!

From outside, someone slid the window open, the new wood barely scratching the frame.

Beneath the quilt, she curled her fingers about the candlestick. As desperately as she wanted to see who the intruder was she squeezed her eyes shut, feigning sleep.

A hand shook her shoulder, gripping hard.

"Mama play ball with baby," she murmured, slurring her speech. She hoped the villain would make a comment and she would recognize his voice.

"A sleep talker, eh?"

Mike! She ought to have known it would be him. Anger snaked through her chest while her heart beat as fast as a trapped bird's.

He leaned close to her ear. His breath smelled like alcohol and sausage. She would have wrinkled her nose in distaste if she hadn't been so deeply "asleep."

"I don't think the talking will trouble Smothers, girlie. You've got other ways of keeping him entertained at night."

She yawned loudly and let the cover slip off one breast. This was not the type of bait she cared to use, but her chest was covered by her shift and this was a desperate situation.

He sucked in his breath. "I reckon the mayor won't mind if I take a squeeze of you since the vows between you all aren't said yet."

"Slimy frog in your pants," she murmured faux-sleepily, then slammed the candlestick against his temple.

Mike crumpled to the floor.

She knelt beside him, quickly searching his pockets for a weapon. The inside pocket of his coat bulged, but not with a gun. She withdrew a wad of money.

Moving quickly, she backed away and counted it.

"Well, Mike, just points out the truth in the old saying, 'crime doesn't pay.'"

She took what he had stolen from her then rained the rest down on his slack-jawed face.

By George, things had worked out well. Here her attacker lay on the floor, just as she had envisioned. He had given back what he had stolen, and as soon as she dashed down the hallway and told Lantree and Grandfather what had happened, they would finally understand that she was well able to take care of herself.

Brimming with the pride of a job well-done and wishing she could tell Melinda all about it she tossed the door open.

"Oh!" She had nearly rushed out without her robe. She spun about to take it off its wall peg.

An arm closed about her throat, squeezing. A fat belly pressed against her derriere.

"See here." The speaker was not the one holding her and making her see stars. "That's no way to treat the woman—"

"Shut your mouth, Smith. I paid you good money to hitch me to this giant. I didn't ask for your opinion."

Her assailant let go of her. She spun about, not surprised to discover that she was glaring at Smothers.

The mayor gazed down at Mike, cursed, then nudged his ribs with the toe of his boot. At least one villain would be out for a good while.

"I will not marry you."

"You brought the paperwork?" Smothers said to Smith, as though she had not voiced an objection.

"It's here. Legal as can be, but it doesn't appear that the bride is willing."

"Don't matter. I paid you three times what a justice of the peace deserves."

Smith shrugged then set a marriage license, pen and ink bottle on the desk. Apparently these men were all of one mind…right or wrong didn't matter when there was money involved.

"Sign it." Smothers turned to her, his order issued.

"I will not!"

He dragged her to the desk, shoved the pen into her hand and held it by squeezing his fingers about hers and the pen. He guided her fist toward the ink bottle.

The fool did not take into account that she still had a free hand. It was a simple matter to swipe up the ink bottle and dash the contents on Smothers's face.

Ink dripped off the tip of his blackened nose. If her situation weren't so grim, she might snort with laughter.

Lantree walked into the room that he shared with Hershal, shutting the door behind him.

His boss reclined against the headboard with his legs crossed at the ankles, his bushy brows creased in a frown.

A man, looking tense as a coiled snake, sat in a chair beside the door with a gun pointed at the old man's chest.

"This here is Dimwit," Hershal explained. "He says once Mike brings him word that Smothers has married Rebecca, he'll skedaddle."

"Say…" Dimwit narrowed his eyes, leaning forward in his chair. "Ain't I seen your face on—?"

Lantree cursed, swiped at the chair leg and caught the gun out of Dimwit's hand as the chair toppled.

On his way out the door, Lantree handed off the gun to Hershal.

"Have you ever heard of my late wife?" he heard his boss say while he rounded the doorway. "Good, because—"

He didn't hear the rest of the ghoulish plans that Mrs. Moreland had in store for Dimwit.

Within five seconds, he reached Rebecca's door, kicked it open and crashed into the room.

He surveyed the scene without slowing his stride.

Harley Smith stood before Smothers, looking as professional as a man could while wearing his nightcap.

Smothers had odd black splotches on his face. Next to Smothers, Rebecca sat in a straight-backed wooden chair, her arms and legs tied to the slats. She wore a frilly sleeping gown, and for some reason she clutched a wad of money in one fist.

"I'd rather marry a worm!" Her eyes spit as much venom as her mouth.

Leaping over Mike, who lay unconscious on the floor, he raced past Rebecca then snagged the mayor by his coat collar and the seat of his pants. He tossed him through the open window. Being a wide man, he hit the top of the frame and broke some glass. Long, razor-like shards shattered on the floor.

With all that went on in Coulson at night, this act went unnoticed.

He spotted a marriage license on the desk. It had Smothers's signature on it. Where Rebecca's should have been was a smear, the ink still glistening. Lantree ripped the paper in two, then for good measure ripped it again.

He carried the pieces to the window and tossed them on top of Smothers, who rolled about, slow to find his feet.

"You got another one of those, Smith?"

"This is very irregular," he said. "Is the bride at least willing this time?"

"Read the vows, Mr. Smith," Rebecca said quickly with a glance at the window. "And be quick about it."

Lantree signed the license then put the pen in Rebecca's tied-up hand. He held the paper close enough for her to scribble her signature. Setting the legalities back on the desk, he stood between Rebecca and the window.

He rested his hand on her shoulder. He wanted to take the time to set her loose but Smothers had gained his feet and was trying to wedge himself back through the window.

Hershal barged into the room, weapon in hand. Lantree hadn't heard a gunshot, at least not one in the hotel, so his boss must have left Dimwit with the ghost of Catherine Moreland to deliver justice.

"Wouldn't if I were you." Hershal pointed the gun at Smothers's knee, which had just cleared the sill.

"Do you—" Smith glanced over at the marriage license "—Lantree Boone Walker, take this woman to—"

"I do."

Smith sighed and glanced again at the license.

"Do you, Rebecca Lousie Lane, take this man to have and to—"

"Yes…yes I do."

"Rings?" the justice asked.

As luck would have it the gold band was still in his pocket. He slipped it on Rebecca's finger. She craned her head, trying to see it, but her hands were behind her.

Smothers set up a string of curses but stayed where he was.

"I now pronounce you man and wife." Smith, a bead of sweat dripping down his neck, hightailed it out of the room, the pom-pom on his nightcap swinging with his long stride.

"Kiss your bride, son," Hershal declared, grinning wide.

He gripped the edges of the chair and lifted it. He took an instant to look into Rebecca's eyes. She clutched the edges of the seat for balance, then blinked wide.

The pink bow that held the bodice of her gown together had come loose. The satin ends draped over the swell of her breasts. Dumbfounded groom or not, he could only notice.

Hershal shoved the mayor back out the window frame.

Lantree yanked the chair close, leaned in and kissed his stunned and no doubt reluctant bride.

Chapter Eleven

Three days on the trail toward home and Rebecca remained stunned.

The fact that she was married, as legal a wife as any had ever been, was a shock all by itself. But what left her half-speechless was the memory of Lantree lifting her from the floor…tied to a chair.

He hadn't grunted or strained, he'd simply plucked up her up as though she weighed no more than Melinda did.

By the saints!

Sitting in the wagon beside Grandfather, she stared at Lantree's back while he led them into the yard in front of the house. She had no idea a man could be so strong.

And here he was, in a sense, hers. How was she to act now?

The one thing she did know was that she was

grateful to be home. The only thing she wanted to do was climb the stairs to her room, collapse upon her bed and come to terms with what had happened.

At least now that they were married, they would no longer have to pretend to be in love. That was a relief…it most certainly was!

She had never meant to marry, and neither had Lantree. But circumstances had changed in a hurry. There had been no time to think, to consider the consequences.

In the moment, they both understood what needed to be done. There had been no choice… no decision to be agonized over.

The ceremony happened quickly. The memory of it flashed in her mind as a blur. All except the kiss.

That kiss had stunned her. Her, well, her husband—that was what he was after all—had lingered over it longer than it had taken to rush through the vows.

The kiss had begun quick and hard, just like everything else leading up to the moment, but then it softened, deepened, made her feel like she was floating…possibly because that was exactly what she was doing.

Subtly, the pressure on her mouth had

changed. Lantree had begun to nip at her lips. She'd grown half-dizzy and then had felt his tongue— *Oh, my.*

In the end, a bucket of cold reality had doused the moment when Mike had begun to stir and Smothers to curse outside the window, vowing that they would all be sorry. Vowing it with ugly words.

What she could not help but wonder was what did Smothers think he could do to a man who lifted a woman tied to a chair as though she were a feather drifting on the breeze?

Early on she had likened Lantree to a massive Viking. Now she thought it even more.

With the mayor's outrage grating on their ears, the three of them had hurried to the livery, gathered the wagon and the horses and fled Coulson by the light of a rising moon.

Naturally, Grandfather grinned all the way home. He had gotten exactly what he'd wanted.

And, truth be told, she could not help but take a few peeks at her wedding ring, the metal glowing softly gold in the moonlight.

She and Lantree had found little to say to each other. Utter shock had stolen their voices, was what she reckoned.

Still, there was a good bit that needed to be

said. Now that a few days had passed to let matters settle in their minds, now that they were safe at home, they would be able to figure a way out of this mess.

Lantree had no wish to be married any more than she did. To add to the trouble, Dimwit had seen Boone's face on the wanted poster.

For his own safety, Lantree would need to be on his way, and in a hurry.

Imagining him riding away, his only belongings those he could carry in his saddle packs, made her heart twist. He had become a friend…a very special friend. It was not fair that he should be forced to move from the home that he loved.

It wasn't right and her heart ached for him.

"Good to be home," Grandfather declared, then got down from the wagon, grinning at her while he stretched. "I'll have Tom and Jeeter bring your things over to Lantree's cabin."

Her gaze locked with Lantree's. She felt her eyes go wide, her body go cold as stone.

A woodpecker tapped at a tree overhead. She heard the front door open and Barstow's boots cross the porch.

This could not be. As soon as she recovered her voice she would say so.

Grandfather announced the good news about

the marriage to the cook as though it really were good news.

"No, Grandfather," she gasped. "Lantree and I, we aren't really married. We never meant to—"

"Hush, now, girl." Grandfather gave her a hand down from the wagon, which she accepted because she felt topsy-turvy. "You are as married as me and my Catherine were, and a sight more married than your parents."

Lantree handed his horse off to Jeeter, who had come running when he heard the wagon roll in.

She waited for Lantree to protest Grandfather's decree, but he stood silently by, staring at the ground and crunching a dirt clod with the toe of his boot.

Well, someone needed to say something rational.

"Don't forget the other thing that happened in Coulson," she pointed out with utmost reason. "Dimwit matched the poster of Boone to Lantree."

Lantree nodded, still silent and grinding the clod to dust.

"He's got to leave…the sooner the better," she pointed out.

"No." Lantree looked up, his blue eyes intent upon her. He walked over to her and placed his big, solid hands on her shoulders. "Rebecca, I'm staying."

"Have you lost your mind?" Of course he had! "You've got to go."

"I've got a wife to protect."

She squinted her eyes at him as though he were a naughty child because he was not making any sense. "Not really. Besides, I'll not have your arrest on my conscience."

"I take full responsibility for my own safety."

"That doesn't mean you have to take responsibility for mine."

"See you lovebirds at dinner." Hershal gave a satisfied nod then walked past Barstow and into the house. "Or maybe not?"

The cook bobbed down the front steps and wrapped her in a great hug. He smelled like onions and garlic.

Ordinarily, she would have been eager to know what delicious thing he was preparing for the evening meal. Just now she thought she might never eat again.

When Barstow finally finished with his hugs and congratulations, Lantree took her hand firmly in his.

"Let's go home, Mrs. Walker," he said, but there was no warmth in the invitation, only resignation.

By George, she was not giving in so easily. She wrenched free of Lantree's grip.

She gathered up her skirt then ran into the house and up the stairs. Once in her room she slammed the door closed.

From down below she heard Screech calling her name. With a groan of frustration she fell belly-first on the bed then covered her head with a pillow.

Even under the fluff, she heard determined footsteps mounting the stairs.

She would be secure in her own room...for about thirty more seconds, since her door had no lock on it.

Four hours later, an easy night rain pattered against the cabin windows.

Rebecca had not spoken a word to him since he'd carried her over his shoulder to his cabin.

Their cabin, he corrected in his mind. She was his wife now. Everything that he had was hers.

"Rebecca."

She stared at the rain dripping down the glass as though he had not spoken. He did not believe that she was being deliberately petulant. That was not the kind of woman she had shown herself to be.

She reached for her violin and began to play a slow, sad-sounding tune.

No, he reckoned she was in shock. It might take some time for her to come to terms with the fact that her life had been upended and there was not a damned thing she could do about it.

"Rebecca, it's time for bed."

The bow squealed across the strings. She spun about on her chair to look at him with narrowed eyes. She didn't look alarmed, but she did look ten kinds of stubborn.

"If you allow me to go back to my own room, I'll be more than happy to go to bed."

"From now on, that—" he inclined his head toward what used to be his bedroom "—is your room."

"I think not."

She stood up, set aside her instrument, then began to pace. She stopped at the bedroom door, gazing in at the bed. When she turned to face him again, she was blushing.

"I aim to sleep on the couch, if that's what's got you in a fluster."

"I'm not in a fluster… All right, maybe I am,

but it's because I don't feel married." She wrung her hands in front of her, twisting her fingers over her rings. "I heard the justice of the peace, I recited vows…but—"

She crossed the room then sat back down on the chair with a flounce, looking frustrated.

"I know it all happened too fast," he said. "But we did what needed doing. Now we've got to make the best of the situation."

She shook her head. "This was supposed to be for show. I don't know why it can't continue to be that way. What, really, has changed except that we said some words in front of Mr. Smith?"

Something had the hell and damn changed for him. Vows had been recited, the certificate signed. He had a wife. He was legally and morally bound to her…to keeping her safe. There was no going back from that.

"Those weren't just any words. They unite us for good or ill… I hope you'll come to find it for the good, Becca."

"Grandfather will be safe at any rate."

He couldn't say that her comment didn't hurt. He'd offered an olive branch and she had dodged it.

"Weren't we friends before we went to Coulson? Can't we be that at least?" he asked.

She closed her eyes and bent her head. When she looked up, her cheeks were moist.

"We can...I'm sorry. You can't be happy with what has happened any more than I am. You, even less so." The moisture that dampened her eyelashes dripped down her cheeks. "I've invaded your house, taken your bed and robbed you of your privacy."

"I always wanted a pretty wife," he said lightly, trying to lighten the mood, but the sudden darkening of her expression told him he had made a mistake.

Well, by damn, if he wanted to call his wife pretty, he was going to.

He stooped beside her chair and stroked the tears from her cheeks with his thumb.

"Becca, you are a lovely woman," he said softly. "Why do you get so angry whenever I say so?"

"Because I know it's not true. When you pay me an empty compliment, it's the same as making fun of me."

"I know beauty when I see it...and don't you believe that I would ever make light of your feelings."

"Maybe you're a flirt. Compliments are a game to you."

"I'm not a flirt." No one had ever accused him of that before. His wife was trying to wriggle her way around the topic.

"I'd like to know why you feel that you are not attractive," he said, going to the heart of the matter.

She was silent for a long time. Then she got up, went to the window and stared out at the rain.

"You've heard of the ugly duckling? The great awkward fowl that grew up among the pretty little chicks?"

"Can't see how that applies."

"Oh, it does… That was my life if you insist on knowing."

"What I remember is that the story ends with a beautiful swan."

"Be that as it may, no one has ever compared me to a swan."

"They have now."

She glanced down at him and the distressed expression on her face ripped his heart.

"My own mother liked her dolls better than she…" He watched the muscles of her throat constrict. "Did you know, Lantree, that back in Kansas City it was whispered about that if I did marry, it would be because some unlucky man was in a desperate situation?"

She glanced down at him, sudden grief darkening her olive eyes. "Oh…a desperate situation is exactly what happened."

"That is not at all what happened."

Lantree rose from where he remained crouched beside the chair then joined her at the window. He touched her shoulders, turned her to look at her reflection in the glass.

"Tell me what you see," he said.

"Rain."

"I see someone lovely." He knew she saw their reflections because she glanced at him in the glass, her expression wary. "I see a woman who can look at me and not be focused on the third button of my shirt. Look here, Becca, if you tip your head to the side—" he cupped her cheek in his hand, pressing gently "—you can rest your head on my shoulder."

"That hardly makes me lovely, Lantree," she said, but she didn't lift her head.

"I'll tell you a secret. I've never even spoken this out loud. I was relieved when my fiancée left me."

She turned so that they no longer looked at each other in the glass.

"You didn't care for her?"

"I did, very much, at first. She seemed to

be everything a man could want, pretty, petite, sweet-natured. After a while, though, I felt her withdraw when we were alone. It turns out, she was afraid of me...of my size. The truth is, when we were intimate she trembled. So I held back, worried that I might hurt her. Then the fever came to town. I couldn't save her parents, and her brother was gone before I knew he was ill. She blamed me."

"For an illness that you didn't cause? That you risked your own life trying to stop? If you ask me, she didn't deserve you. You were a hero, Lantree, flat out and plain."

All of a sudden she hugged him around the middle. He felt the tickle of her hair under his chin.

"I'm sorry it didn't work out for you."

"Don't be. Eloise and I would never have suited." He kissed the top of her head, felt her take a long breath and lean into him. "The reason I'm telling you all this is so you'll know how special you are. Tiny women might be what society sets as the standard, but to me, you are the beautiful one. And while you are beautifully formed, loveliness goes so much deeper in you, Becca. You are smart and resourceful, brave and funny. When I look at you I hear music, even when you're not playing your violin. So when I tell you that you are beautiful, I'm seeing you inside as well as out…and I'm being sincere when I say so."

"Well—" she placed her hands on his chest and shoved away from him "—at any rate, we have bigger issues to face than my appearance."

His words had not convinced her that she was not the ugly duckling. But he had opened his heart to her and he could only hope that in time it would make a difference.

"I suggest we take them one at a time," he said.

"I suppose that's the only way we'll get by."

"Will you agree to sleep in the bed if I sleep on the couch?"

"That hardly seems fair. This is your home."

It was his home and he'd been happy living in it by himself.

No longer, though. Now that she was here he knew this sturdy cabin was where she belonged, where he wanted her to be.

"I want you here, Becca. Please say you'll stay. We can work things out as we go along."

She nodded then walked toward the bedroom. She turned.

"We can remain friends, Lantree, and I'm glad

for it." She shut the bedroom door behind her and he was left staring at the polished wood.

He wondered if that bit about friendship was true. He could not say exactly when things had changed for him, but what he wanted was a wife. He wanted his sweet and spirited Rebecca.

Rebecca opened the front door of the cabin, letting the morning light stream inside. She went to each window doing the same. She breathed in a deep lungful of fresh summer air.

Three weeks had passed and the world had not quit spinning because she was married. It was true that hers was not a marriage in the typical sense, but she and Lantree had worked out a living arrangement that worked for them.

They shared the house, but not the bedroom. He rose early to light the fire, then banked it again at night. She laundered and mended his clothes.

Most nights they went to the main house for dinner and companionship, but other nights they kept to their own company, staying up late, laughing and talking like friends would do.

She would not have believed it possible on that first night when Lantree had carted her over here, but this snug little cabin was beginning to seem like home.

It had taken a while to get used to the idea of living with a man who she did not really feel married to. It felt a bit wicked, even though in the eyes of everyone but her it was perfectly respectable.

Leaning her elbows on the windowsill she gazed down the slope at the paddock, watching Lantree while he went about his morning chores.

She liked watching him, the way his muscles moved under his shirt when he worked, the way he touched the animals with a gentle hand.

When it came to her husband, her emotions were a jumble. Things were comfortable between them, but at the same time tense.

Mostly, they behaved like lifelong friends. Those were comfortable times. But other times, when he thought she did not notice, he would look at her in a peculiar way. A way that made her itch inside.

If she were to be perfectly honest, she enjoyed that curious feeling. Sometimes she would awake in the middle of the night and listen to Lantree breathing from the front room. She would toss and turn, wonder about things.

Things like what was acceptable in an unintended marriage.

If she were to do something scandalous like... oh, say, strip bare and parade naked before him, it would be to her mind perfectly wicked when in fact, according to the ways of marriage, it would not be.

Those and similar thoughts plagued her during the night and lately even during the day, when she found herself watching him from a distance like she was doing now.

What a ninny she was, imagining things that could never be. If they ever did become married in the way marriage was intended, attachments would form.

He'd told her a few times that he had no intention of leaving this ranch, Boone or no Boone. But that was foolishness.

And to boot, if life went the way of her daydreams, there might be a child.

All of a sudden, it felt like her heart rolled over on itself. A baby...for her?

By the saints, what a silly thing she was. She would not be giving Lantree Walker a son or a daughter. What made her think he would even want that?

She shook herself, regaining her emotional balance. Doing something creative would set her right. First she sat for a moment with her violin. She played something quick and levelheaded sounding. Nothing daydreamy this morning.

Next, she decided to set her hand to something practical. A big batch of freshly baked cookies ought to make the work in the corral more pleasant on this quickly warming day.

She went to the main house and, while baking the cookies, spent a pleasant hour with Barstow as he prepared the midday meal.

Treats in hand, she walked toward the barn and saw the men gathered, taking a break from the heat in the shade of the big trees in the paddock.

Grandfather, Tom and Jeeter sat on tree stumps. As was becoming more common with each passing day, they glanced at her belly before greeting her with a smile.

Surely they did not think that in three weeks' time her stomach would suddenly swell. How disappointed they would be if they knew that Baby Walker was never going to be.

Lantree, having fed Fancy Francie and her growing calves, crossed the paddock toward her, a smile on his handsome face.

Day by day, she was coming to love that smile, the way it would flash so suddenly and light up his expression.

"Hot damn, Lantree!" Jeeter exclaimed, jumping up and slapping his thigh. "Not even midday and here comes your missus with tidbits from heaven."

Luckily, she had made more than enough, knowing that Jeeter ate more than three grown men would.

She sat down on a stump and handed the cookies to the men while behind her, Lantree leaned against the rail fence. She handed a couple of cookies back to him.

While the men munched, they discussed local events.

Apparently, Coulson was not the only place where railroad fever was heating up.

"We're all going to Billings, aren't we?" Jeeter asked, crumbs dotting his lips. "This is an historic event."

"Someone's got to mind the ranch," she pointed out, hoping that the one to remain behind would be Lantree. The farther away he stayed from the strangers who would be thronging in, the safer he would be.

"We could hire the Fulton boys. Their pa's always eager for them to make some extra money. And the boys like to get away from home now and again," Grandfather said. "And since Barstow doesn't like to travel, he'll be here."

"But what about—"

"Jeeter's right," Lantree cut her off, probably sensing that she was looking for a way to keep him at home. "Things are going to change in these parts. I want to witness the beginning."

"Ain't we due for a supply trip about then, anyway?" Tom put in.

"It'll be a grand sight, seeing that big old locomotive rolling over the track, belching out steam and smoke," Grandfather declared.

"I reckon there's got to be some settlers coming who have daughters." Jeeter slapped his knee, clearly pleased with the prospect.

"When do we leave?" Rebecca asked resigned.

The fact was, she was as anxious as anyone to watch the train pull in for the first time. Not only that, it had been said that Billings was growing fast, soon to be bigger than Coulson.

The mayor must be in a fit over that state of events.

"Three weeks," Lantree announced, looking nearly as pleased as Jeeter did.

The thought of being so close to Coulson jittered her nerves, but she could not deny that she was anxious to witness the arrival of the train and the new town growing up around it.

Chapter Twelve

There was a holiday feel about the trip to Billings. Rebecca was half-glad that she had not had the chance to talk the men out of going.

They camped at the same lovely, secluded spot where she had secretly bathed. In a way it was a shame they would only spend one night.

The day was settling into twilight and she walked about under the trees gathering small kindling for the campfire. Tom and Jeeter had gone deeper into the woods to gather logs. Grandfather unloaded the wagon, tossing out cans of beans, blankets and brushes for grooming the horses.

Lantree watered the animals at the pond. He seemed to be looking at something in the water, toward the center. Whatever it was, she did not see it.

Bringing the horses back to the campsite, a

grin cut across his face. His gaze slowly swept her from head to toe.

How curious.

"Have you spotted a big fat trout for our dinner?" she asked, because what else would he have seen?

His grin tweaked up on one side. "I do have an appetite all of a sudden."

An hour later, it was full dark, the sky alive with stars.

The night had cooled so the campfire felt nice. The five of them sat about the snapping flames eating fish off the bone.

The evening's conversation touched on many things but always it came back to the arrival of the railroad…how it would change things for good and for ill.

Grandfather asked for a serenade so she unwrapped her violin from the padding she had protected it with and began to play. She started with something lively to express the excitement over the coming train.

As the evening deepened, and a quieter mood set in, Grandfather made a request.

"Becca, won't you play 'Canon in D'? It was your grandmother's favorite and I haven't heard it since—" His voice caught. "Well, for a very long time."

While she played, the night seemed to slow down. The song of crickets and frogs faded. She felt Lantree's gaze lingering upon her. Her blood felt slow and languid in her veins.

In the silence that followed the piece, she wanted to say that there was another person around the campfire. That she had felt Catherine Moreland's fingers lightly on top of her own, but in the moment a human voice would sound intrusive.

Grandfather surely thought so. Without a word, he rose from his spot by the campfire and went to his bedroll.

Moments later Jeeter and Tom stood, yawned, then nodded a good evening.

Within moments the snoring began.

After a while, her head began to sag. Lantree caught her hands and helped her up from the ground. He snatched up the wool blanket they had been sitting upon then wrapped it around her shoulders. He drew her close to him by pulling on the fringed hem.

Golden light from the campfire reflected on his face. No doubt about it, she had married an exceptionally handsome man.

This close, his eyes no longer appeared blue. They reflected the amber blaze of the flames.

She felt downright singed by the look he leveled upon her. Her feminine parts had gone feverish…simmering in a curiously pleasurable way.

She had no experience to know that this was true, but she suspected that this feeling, left unchecked, would lead to something she could never come back from.

The prospect frightened and delighted her at the same time. She could not deny that his gaze, so hot and possessive upon her, made her feel a little bit married.

"You look so damn pretty by firelight, Becca. You can be angry if you want to, but I've been waiting to tell you for some time."

She wanted to be offended, but she seemed to have temporarily misplaced that emotion. Perhaps because he had called her Becca again. He was doing that more often lately and she could not deny the tug it gave her heart.

"You have a right to your opinion," she declared, because she needed to say something but wasn't sure what it should be.

A wolf howled not far in the distance. An owl hooted on a branch overhead while small creatures scurried in the brush.

"Sleep with me tonight."

With all the wildlife stirring in the dark, the

idea was appealing. She had wanted to suggest the same thing last night, but could not work up the nerve.

"For safety's sake," she mumbled.

"Because I want to feel you beside me." He tugged the blanket tighter, pressing her close to his chest.

"Oh…well then."

He slipped his arm about her waist, led her close to the water's edge where, earlier, he had set up the bedrolls.

He knelt and rearranged the separate beds into one.

Fully clothed, she lay down between the blankets. Lantree slipped in beside her.

The man was a flame. His warmth seeped past her clothing, heating her to the bone. Thank goodness she would not spend the night shivering. How strange it was that the days in these parts could be so warm yet the nights so cold.

For a long time she watched the stars, listening to the rumbles and snorts of the men who slept about the campfire.

Lantree also watched the stars, his head tipped so that she felt the tickle of his hair on her ear. After a while, he turned his face and she watched his gaze settle on her.

She drew in a quick breath. The emotion she saw in his eyes was not that of a comfortable friend. He was a man, wanting a woman…wanting his woman.

He touched her hair, smoothing back some of the tangles that the day's ride had caused.

"My sweet, beautiful Becca," he whispered.

There might be words in the universe to chastise that remark, but at this moment she could not find them…did not want to.

His breath skimmed her forehead, slid down her nose, then huffed against her mouth.

A kiss, warm and featherlight, came down upon her lips. The scent of Lantree filled her senses. The taste of him made her melt into the kiss instead of shy from it as good sense warned her to.

The problem was, over the weeks her feelings for him had grown. She would be a fool to deny that her emotions had not morphed from friendship into something more intimate.

The draw of what was forbidden sent a delicious shiver through her because forbidden was something that existed only in her mind.

His tongue touched her lips, gentle, coaxing until she opened for him.

She felt his fingers at her waist, tugging her

shirt out of her riding skirt. The fabric of her camisole shifted then his fingers were against her bare skin, stroking and petting while they crept deliberately up her ribs.

His kisses moved from her lips to her jaw, then to her neck where her pulse thudded.

She made a sound that she had never made in her life, a soft moan…for something. She wasn't certain what it was, but it was wicked and she wanted it.

"Rebecca." The heat of his breath, so sultry and masculine, brushed her skin. She shivered.

The calloused fingers of a cowboy, gentled by a physician's touch, stroked the flesh over her ribs, lingering for an instant here and a moment there, but there was no mistaking where they intended to go.

Now was when she ought to call on reason, to roll up in a blanket and sleep alone.

In the distance, wolves called to one another, sounding lonely. The mournful howls went on for a long time, then after a short yip, became silent.

Tonight, unlike the wolves, she was not going to be lonely.

When Lantree's fingers fondled the under curve of her breast, she arched into his touch.

She heard his sharp intake of breath, then his muffled moan when he pressed his palm over the full swell of her flesh.

He squeezed her, gently kneading, tugging her nipple between his finger and thumb, then slipping his hand sideways, caressed her other breast.

Forbidden fruit, forbidden fruit, forbidden fruit! She repeated it over and over in her mind, but that only made her want to taste it fully.

What would it be like to feel the warm moist heat of his mouth tugging where his fingers plucked and gently twisted? All of a sudden she wanted that knowledge more than anything.

Her heartbeat raced, she panted and there was not a single thing she could do to control it.

Lantree withdrew his hands from under her camisole with a quiet groan.

It was only then that she noticed that the crickets had fallen silent and footsteps were approaching the pond.

From a short distance away came a relieved sigh, then the sound of a stream of urine pelting weeds. After a moment, the footsteps went back the way they had come.

Lantree turned her away from him but then

tugged her close once more, spooning his big Viking body about hers.

She snuggled backward, cherishing the moment.

"The time's coming, Rebecca. I intend to make you my wife in every way. Just not out here with a bunch of snoring cowboys to witness." He kissed the top of her head. "Sleep now, love."

With what had happened, she would have sworn that to be impossible but when her eyes blinked open, it was nearly dawn and Grandfather was tending to the horses.

Heavy clouds pressed heat close to the ground. Rebecca stood beside the railroad tracks, the neck of her blouse growing damp with sweat. Even her hair felt clammy at the roots.

Respectable-size crowds had gathered on both sides of the tracks. Even though the official railroad ceremony would not occur for months, plenty of folks had been of the same mind as the Moreland group. No matter how one felt about it, the arrival of the first train was exciting.

For everyone's sake, she hoped that the train would come on schedule. It couldn't be long before people started fainting from the close air.

Billings was growing fast. All the structures

were new, the lumber still fresh with the scent of resin. Not a stick of it from Moreland land, though. Alongside the new construction, tents were erected, folks ready to do business even before the buildings were finished.

For all its rapid growth, the young town could not accommodate everyone who had come to greet the train.

Not wanting to stay in Coulson, Lantree had found them a shady campsite beside the river. Other ranchers had done the same.

Many of them knew Grandfather, Lantree and the hands. There had been two nights of pleasant socializing beside the Yellowstone, along with many heartfelt congratulations to the newly-weds.

She had thanked everyone with a smile. Not a forced smile for a pretend marriage, either. To her surprise her thanks was genuine. While she didn't quite feel like a bride, neither did she feel like an imposter.

Just when she had come to accept that she was married, that perhaps she was content with the situation, she could not say.

The kisses had swayed her. There was no denying how much she enjoyed them. But kisses alone would not explain her softened attitude.

The change had to have begun during the nights they spent alone together in the cabin. Bonds of friendship had been formed, then without her being fully aware, deeper feelings must have taken root.

Roots, she reckoned, were a beginning. Most growing things began with roots.

Now, after last night, there was a glow in her chest, and she liked the warmth of it too much to quash it entirely.

It seemed a natural action to slip her hand into her husband's. He stood head and shoulders above everyone.

He seemed pleased by her touch. With a quick kiss on her cheek, he squeezed her hand.

Ah well, life would play out as it would. If a real marriage resulted, she would be happy about it.

All at once the crowd began to murmur. Hands waved and pointed toward the east. Miles away, black smoke became visible. Although the train was still a good distance away, they could hear the whistle blowing.

Fathers lifted small children onto their shoulders while business owners hurried out of buildings and tents.

A dozen or more brightly dressed whores

who had come from Coulson stood in a wagon waving.

In addition to a three-man band on a platform, there was Mayor Smothers and Coulson's wild-looking lawman. Behind them stood railroad officials. One of them was Mr. Billings himself, so the rumors went.

Smothers glanced at the Moreland group a time or two but his gaze slid across her as though she were a stranger. Which…in spite of everything that had happened, she was.

It was unlikely that he had gotten over being shoved out a window, his ridiculous plans thwarted, but maybe he had accepted the fact that she was now a married woman.

At any rate, she felt safe enough with Grandfather flanking her on the right and Lantree on the left, with Tom and Jeeter close by.

When a subtle rumble shook the ground, she forgot about the mayor altogether. The train was coming!

A baby cried. Dogs barked and horses stomped as the huge black engine charged forward on the tracks.

The band played a rousing tune in welcome but the sound was soon drowned out by the clack of metal wheels reverberating on the tracks.

Foolishly, a few men fired guns in celebration. Lantree frowned and moved behind her, then drew her close to his chest. His arms, great bands of muscle, wrapped protectively around her.

Many people eagerly waved small flags.

No matter how things changed for the area, this was a great and exciting moment.

Approaching the train station, the engineer applied the brakes and the whistle. A cloud of steam billowed all around.

One could now see passengers waving their arms out of the windows in excited greeting.

Smiling porters exited the railcars first, helping folks with their bags as they stepped down. There were plenty of families, settlers looking eager to begin new lives, also men wearing suits probably hoping to create new businesses.

Loved ones found each other with tears and embraces. With the coming of the railroad, families would no longer suffer long separations.

A moment after the people began to disembark, the doors of the rear cars opened to unload supplies and livestock.

"This is quite a day." Grandfather raised his voice to be heard above all the activity.

Lantree seemed to be studying each face that

passed by. If she knew him, and she felt she did by now, he would be looking for signs of illness. He had to be concerned that what happened in his former town might happen here.

She found that she was also staring at faces, watching for any flare of recognition that someone had recognized Boone in Lantree.

In her opinion, one that did not seem to be shared among the others, he had put himself in a risky situation so that they could all witness this grand event. The sooner they were on the trail home, the safer he would be.

The safer Grandfather would be, as well. No matter that Smothers seemed uninterested, he made her stomach curl.

She lifted up on her toes, yanked Lantree's hat lower over his face.

"Let's go home," she shouted in his ear.

"We ought to eat first."

No, she couldn't even try, not with all these strangers milling about who might know of Boone. She might dip his hat, but that could not hide his size.

Wherever he went, people's gazes were drawn to him, as they were to her. The pair of them were bound to draw comment.

"We can eat on the way home," she said. "Billings is making me nervous all of a sudden."

"Your wife is right, boy," Grandfather stated in the tone he used when making a no-arguments decree. "We've had our fun and now we'll go home."

"Wouldn't mind a beer first," Jeeter said, with his eyes trained wistfully on the brightly colored doves soliciting the men stepping off the train.

"That's no fit way to get lai—" Tom glanced at Rebecca, his face going suddenly red. "Go hitch and water the team, you young fool."

A movement at the corner of her eye drew Rebecca's attention. Just the swing of a woman's skirt and the set of her shoulders…but it felt familiar. Before she could get more than a fleeting impression, the crowd closed around her.

How odd.

She squeezed Lantree's arm. The rightness of the gesture made her feel sunny inside. Maybe… just perhaps—

"Becca! Becca! Becca!" she heard a voice shout from behind her. This was impossible. It had to be a similar voice calling a similar name. "Rebecca Louise Lane!"

She let go of Lantree's arm then spun about.

"Melinda!"

* * *

The young woman who had called Rebecca's name dropped her bag on the platform and ran forward, her frilly skirt a cloud of blue. Even from this distance he heard her sob of joy.

Beside him Rebecca shrieked, then rushed to meet the girl who he reckoned could only be the cousin she had grown up with.

Melinda grabbed Rebecca about the waist. Rebecca dipped her head to her cousin's shoulder. They cried all over each other for a moment, then stopped and gazed at one another at arm's length.

Lantree walked forward and picked up Melinda's bag where it lay forgotten.

"What are you doing here?" Clearly, Rebecca was still stunned. "I can't believe it!"

"I told you I would shrivel up without you... so here I am."

"You came all by yourself?" Rebecca glanced about and apparently did not spot anyone else she knew. "Why would you do something so dangerous?"

Lantree rolled his eyes. He couldn't help it. Coming to Montana by train was a sight safer than coming by steamboat, to his way of thinking.

"I've been sick with worry this whole time,

Becca. How could I be certain you had even made it here? At least for me there was no danger. Sitting on a bench hour upon endless hour is hardly risky. Unless one dies of boredom, that is."

"But you don't even know where the ranch is! How would you have found me if I hadn't come to see the train?"

He cringed inside. Melinda probably would have done the same thing that his wife had, set out willy-nilly and assume no harm would come to her.

"Of course you'd be here. It's the first train. You would never miss something as grand as that. I was sure you'd be here."

Melinda's gaze left Rebecca for the first time. She glanced at Lantree then the others, who had looks on their faces that ranged from surprise to confusion to admiration.

Jeeter no longer appeared sullen over having been denied the charms of the painted ladies.

And why would he? Melinda Winston was an exceptional beauty. Blonde and petite, with blue eyes that sparkled with humor, a full sensuous mouth that, from all he could see, laughed often. She was a woman who no doubt left a man smitten for the simple reason that she'd smiled at him.

With a sinking heart, Lantree understood what prompted his Becca to feel the way she did about her appearance. Any female standing beside Melinda would feel less of a woman.

For one who felt like an ugly duckling to begin with… Well, damn it, there was more than one ideal of beauty.

For her whole life, Rebecca would have heard the comparisons, from her aunt, from potential beaus and even from strangers.

Curse it, here was Jeeter all but drooling and Tom nearly so. He'd give them a swift kick in the pants if he could do it without anyone asking why.

If it took him the rest of his life, he was going to make Rebecca understand that her beauty was as outstanding as any woman's. To his mind she was the loveliest woman alive, from her soul to her bones to the curve of her smile.

It had become clear that he could not live without her.

"You've found your grandfather!" Melinda walked toward Hershal with her fair, delicate-looking hand extended. "It is a great pleasure to meet you, Mr. Moreland."

Hershal shook her hand but did not stop with that formal greeting. Without letting go of her wrist he wrapped Melinda in a hug.

"I'm glad that you've come, little miss. Our Rebecca has missed you. She speaks of you daily."

After a moment of soaking up the old man's hug, Melinda glanced at the rest of them, clearly anxious for an introduction.

"Melinda, this is Tom Camp," Rebecca said. Tom nodded and shook her hand.

"This is Jeeter Spruce." Jeeter also shook her hand, holding it so reverently that it was obvious that he wanted to kiss it. "Tom and Jeeter work for Grandfather."

Melinda looked up at Lantree, her blue eyes a-twinkle. Something was turning over in her mind but damned if he could tell what.

"And this…" Rebecca took a sidestep toward him. "Well, this is, Lantree Walker…my grandfather's head man."

That introduction left him gut punched.

Not her husband, but Hershal's employee.

The intimacy they'd shared by the pond had meant something to him. It had to her, he'd bet his life on it. He'd seen it in her eyes, heard it in her sigh.

Since then, there had been an attachment between them that had not been there before and he knew damn well he had not imagined it.

At some point Rebecca's cousin was going to learn of the marriage, but it would not be from him. This was something for Rebecca to reveal as she would.

It ate at him, though, wondering if when they returned to the ranch Rebecca would continue to live with him in the cabin.

Melinda's arrival had changed things. The woman hadn't only brought along a big, fully-stuffed trunk. She had brought Rebecca's former life.

Would his wife choose it over him?

It had been her choice to leave Kansas City, but with everything that had happened since she arrived, he couldn't help but wonder if she regretted coming.

She had never wanted marriage…he hadn't, either. But now he did. With all the obstacles it presented, still he wanted it.

Much more than he had with Eloise. He'd been devastated when she left him, but that had more to do with the way she'd left him. She'd publicly announced him a wretched failure then marched away and married someone else before he had even scraped the remains of his heart from the cemetery stones. He couldn't say that once the relationship ended he had truly missed her.

This would not be the case with Rebecca. She was a woman of strength, of compassion. If, for whatever reason, they parted, he would miss her…the woman, her heart and soul and everything that made her who she was.

He wanted this marriage. He only hoped that she felt the same way.

After only two hours on the trail, the oppressive heat of the afternoon gave way to rain. Lightning arched across the sky. Thunder rumbled through the wood slats of the wagon.

Rebecca didn't relish the thought of being caught out in the open during a storm, but that was nothing compared to remaining in town and having her nerves spin like a whirling dervish whenever someone looked overlong at Lantree.

Melinda suggested that they remain in Coulson for the night. She must wonder why her companions were acting so rashly. No one had as yet explained about Smothers or about Boone and the reasons for their haste to get out of town.

Perhaps it was Rebecca's place to tell her…just

like it had been her place to introduce Lantree as her husband.

It's not that she had not wanted to. The joy of her news had been bubbling up in her…until she caught the look on her cousin's face.

Melinda had taken one look at Lantree and fallen in love with him. She knew her cousin too well to not know this was true.

Just now, while she and her cousin rode in the back of the wagon getting caught up on who had done what to who back in Kansas City, she watched Melinda's gaze settle on Lantree's broad back, the fall of blond hair on his shoulders.

A drip of water hit the bag of rice that served as their bench. Grandfather reached behind him, freed a tarp and tossed it back to them.

Rebecca settled it over their heads, shoulders and the rice. Melinda tucked a second cover over their knees and wrapped it about their feet.

Rain tapped on the tarp. She glanced up to see Grandfather and Lantree shrugging into their slickers, hurrying to get settled before the downpour began in earnest.

All in all, the quick shelter that she shared with Melinda was cozy.

"Montana certainly grows some handsome men." Melinda arched a brow. "And tall."

Yes, tall and handsome…strong yet gentle, compassionate, heroic…

She wanted to jump off the wagon and drown in the mud because, if it had not been for Melinda's sudden arrival, she would have shared Lantree's bed the moment they got home.

The desire to know him in a carnal way hummed below the surface of her skin. It made her want to stretch like a cat in the sun, but at the same time it made her nervous, touchy in her woman parts.

But here Melinda was, and with a twinkle in her eye. Rebecca knew from experience that no man could resist that twinkle.

"No wonder you are in love, Becca. This beautiful country goes straight to your heart."

She nodded because if she spoke she would weep.

Of course, she could tell Melinda that Lantree was her husband and she loved him, but what good would it do?

Years ago, she had been enamored of a young man, and he had showed some interest in her… but only until he met Melinda. One innocent smile from her cousin and the fellow fell hard. That's how it always went. Melinda was joyful sunshine and Rebecca her long shadow.

Within a few days Lantree would be in love, too. Just in love with Melinda.

There was nothing she wanted more than Melinda's happiness, unless it was Lantree's.

It was after dark and still raining when Lantree called a halt to the day's travel.

They didn't bother with a fire, just ate some hardtack to curb their hunger.

When Lantree set up the bedrolls, he put hers and Melinda's under the wagon. He lay down under a tree with the other men.

While it was wonderful spending the night with her cousin, laughing, gossiping and catching up, she well and truly missed lying in the safe circle of Lantree's arms.

It broke her heart wondering if the reason he had set up their bedrolls yards apart was that perhaps he was already reconsidering his wish to make their marriage real.

Or maybe she had broken his heart by not introducing him as her husband.

Life was certainly confusing at the moment and since she could not do anything to make it happen one way or another, she said, "Good night, cousin. I'm glad you came."

"Me, too, Becca... I've missed you."

Rebecca closed her eyes, listening to the

sounds of the men's breathing, easily identifying which quiet snore was Lantree's.

Life would play out as it would…not particularly how she would wish it to.

Chapter Thirteen

A tree limb snapped. Lantree heard the crack of splintering wood, then the thud of the weight hitting the ground.

Melinda Winston screamed.

He abandoned the horses drinking at the stream and bounded up the bank, his heart pounding against his ribs.

Miss Winston lay on the ground with Rebecca kneeling beside her. Hershal, Jeeter and Tom all broke the perimeter of the woods at the same time, dropping firewood in their haste to reach camp.

Lantree was the first man to reach the scene. He knelt beside the fallen woman. She gazed up at him from under the broken branch, her eyes wide and, no doubt about it, angry.

"Never, ever, have I had a branch go out from under me."

"You are a long way from Missouri," Rebecca admonished her cousin. "Things are very different here…birds do have mothers to get them out of trouble."

"Well, Mrs. Feather must have dozed off… and her poor baby not even able to fly yet. Didn't you see some sort of a creature creeping up on the helpless little thing? Where is it anyway?"

Glancing about, Melinda attempted to wriggle out from under the log but she yelped and lay back down.

"It flew away—" Rebecca caught Lantree's eye and nodded toward Melinda's leg "—with its red-tailed mother."

The rest of the men came upon the scene winded and worried looking.

With care, they all lifted the branch and set it aside.

"I believe I'll need a doctor," Melinda said, with a fine sheen of perspiration beginning to dampen her forehead.

Finally, the woman had the good grace to look sensibly frightened.

"You'll be happy to know that my… That Lantree is a physician." Rebecca held his gaze and gave him a firm nod. "A very fine one, too.

He stitched up my foot and it won't even leave a scar."

He glanced sharply at his wife. She dropped her gaze. Why had she come so close to identifying him as her husband and then not?

He ran his fingers lightly along Melinda's calf, over her stocking. Thank the Good Lord that the break was slight, that he would not have to look into Rebecca's eyes and tell her that her cousin was in a risky condition.

He glanced at Hershal, giving him a nod.

"Let's get back to our wood gathering, men," he announced.

When they had their backs respectfully turned, he asked Rebecca to roll down Melinda's stocking. She did that then lifted her cousin's frilly petticoat past her knee. The flesh had already begun to swell and bruise.

"I'm afraid there's a fracture, about halfway between your knee and ankle, but not a horrible one."

He smiled to give her reassurance. In this case it was valid and for the first time in a long while he felt the love for healing scratching at his gut.

"Mother can never know about this," Melinda said with a pleading glance at Rebecca.

"There are a great many things about living

in these parts that your mother would be happier not knowing."

Again, Rebecca glanced at him, but this time he swore that she shot him a brief conspiratorial smile.

Just now he'd take any sort of smile she offered. He'd give a lot to know what had changed her mind about the tenuous bond they had formed.

He could only hope that seeing Melinda again hadn't made her long for the easier life that she'd had in Kansas City.

"Let's get you home, Miss Melinda," he said. "It's not the worst break I've ever set, but you'll feel better once you are under a proper roof and in a proper bed."

It only took another full day to reach Moreland Ranch. It might have taken longer but the weather turned good and the roads were no longer muddy.

Once home, Tom carried Melinda up the stairs and into the main house. With the front door open he heard Barstow exclaiming and clucking hen-like over the new, injured arrival.

Rebecca waited behind, turning to Lantree when everyone else had gone inside.

"I hope you aren't doubting yourself, Lantree.

I know how brilliant you are at healing." She glanced at the open front door, then back at him. For all her encouraging words, she seemed agitated. "Well…"

Here was the moment he had anticipated…or dreaded. Would she continue to live with him or not?

"I think," she said, wringing her hands in front of her, "that Melinda is going to need me. She'll need care at all hours, much of which you men would not be comfortable offering."

She was right, of course, but… "You're moving out?"

"For the time being. My cousin needs nursing…you understand?"

He shoved a bothersome hank of loose hair behind his ear. "What I understand is that since she got off the train something has changed… between us."

He wasn't imagining the moisture welling in her eyes.

"Yes, well, Melinda is special. She changes people, they fall in love with her and can't…" She swiped at her cheek. "Can't help it."

"I'll admit she's charming, but—" He didn't get to finish what he wanted to say because she turned and fled toward the house.

"I'll be in directly to check on her," he called.

* * *

"And so," Melinda said, with two pillows propped behind her head and three more elevating her splinted leg, "the butcher was none too pleased when he discovered that Rebecca had fled. He came pounding at our door at ten-twenty-two in the evening. It caused quite a lot of attention among the neighbors, which, as you can imagine, Mama hated."

As far as Rebecca could tell, Lantree was entertained by the story while he went about the business of checking Melinda's leg. Every now and then he looked up from what he was doing to nod and smile.

Rebecca had already told Lantree about the butcher and about her own tangled relationship with Aunt Eunice.

"You should have seen it, Becca! Mama got out the broom and waved it at him, like she was sweeping filth from her stoop. Then Mr. Portlet from next door charged over the fence with the flap of his long johns hanging by one button— we can only guess that he came directly from the outhouse when he heard the commotion. Now, I can't say for certain since I came here before I had absolute proof, but I believe that Mr. Portlet is sweet on Mama and she has taken a hankering for him."

That was a surprise, indeed! She could not help but say so. Even Lantree raised a brow.

"I say this because she baked him a spice cake, and not only that but when I told her I was going to Montana to be with you, her fainting spell only lasted ten seconds."

"How long do you intend to stay, Melinda?" Lantree asked.

Her cousin looked at Lantree, her smile sweet and becoming. "I'd like to see how things develop."

Then she slid her gaze to Rebecca. "This is an amazing country, cousin. I'll stay as long as you'll have me."

What Melinda likely meant was that she wanted to see if Lantree had, or would, fall in love with her.

At some point she would have to reveal that they were married. She loved her cousin too much to let her become attached to a married man.

At least, married for now. Perhaps once they knew that Grandfather would remain safe—or that Lantree did not have to seek a safer place— she could have the marriage annulled.

So far she had not done anything to make that impossible.

All of a sudden she felt sick to her stomach

because she could not tell which was worse, the two people she loved most in the world being together or not being together.

She rose from her chair all of a sudden.

"I've got to check on my calves."

Rushing to the door she could not rid herself of the image of Lantree's fingers touching Melinda's forehead, grazing her cheek.

Clearly he was merely feeling for signs of a fever, but still, the sight hurt.

As much as she wanted to deny it, her big, strapping husband and her pretty, petite cousin made a fine-looking pair.

Lantree Walker was the very man, Rebecca was certain, that her cousin had been waiting for all these years.

Melinda was never meant to be a spinster.

Until lately, Rebecca had believed that she was destined to that fate. Perhaps it would not be so difficult to slip back into the role.

If only she could forget that she had married the man that she, herself, had been waiting for.

And that she loved him.

On a sunny afternoon in early September, Melinda leaned on the crutch that Tom had fashioned for her. She cooed to and petted Mocha.

As far as Rebecca could tell, no one had mentioned her marriage to Lantree.

Rightly so. They probably considered it her business to do it. And she would…one day very soon.

She had meant to do it the first day home, then last week, but the time never felt right and the more time that passed the less right it felt.

And, to be honest, she didn't want to.

Still, last night she had nearly done it, even had the first word of confession on her tongue, while she and Melinda sat alone on the porch listening to the crickets and frogs.

But just then Lantree had come out of the house and asked her to go walking with him. She'd hesitated until Melinda yawned a great yawn, stretched and declared that she could not keep her eyes open one more minute.

They had walked to the paddock, sat and talked of this and that, then come back to the house. He'd held her hand, which made her feel elated…and guilty.

Maybe she should go back to Kansas City where life was predictable and emotions were uncluttered…where snowcapped mountains did not kiss the sky and where the wind did not whisper through treetops so tall one could hardly see the tips.

Where Grandfather's smile did not greet her every morning and his kiss on her cheek did not send her off to bed...where calf noses, soft as velvet, did not nudge her palm in search of a treat.

She brought herself up short, knowing she would never leave this ranch. All she was doing was feeling sorry for herself when she ought to be rejoicing over Melinda's good fortune.

"Becca." She felt something tickle her nose. With a start, she saw that Melinda stood before her, stabbing her with a blade of straw. "Where have you been these past weeks? Ever since I got here you've seemed different...sad and not like yourself at all."

Now was the time to speak if ever there was one.

Francie mooed. Rebecca stroked the cow's soft ears, choosing her words.

"There's something that you might need to know," she began. "It has to do with Lantree... or his brother more likely."

"That outlaw, Boone, you mean?" Melinda sat down on a hay bale so Rebecca settled beside her. "Tom told me about that. It's such a sad story...poor Lantree being denied his brother's companionship all these years."

"Has Tom told you anything else?"

Melinda arched a brow at her. "That you snatched Boone's likeness off the sheriff's wall."

Evidently, Tom had not told her about the marriage.

"Becca, what do you think of him?"

"I like Tom very much," Rebecca answered.

"I don't mean Tom and I think you know that. Lantree, what do you think of him?"

He's my husband and I love him. And I ought to fight for him. That thought startled her… Fight for him against Melinda?

She loved her cousin far too much to stand in the way of her happiness. Besides, even if she tried, she would be no match.

"He's kind…and he's very devoted to my Grandfather."

"I think he's handsome. Don't you recall the dream man we made up when we were young? It's him if anyone is." Melinda cocked her head to one side, studying her intently. "He will make some lucky woman a wonderful husband."

This was her chance to give them her blessing but instead, she said, "Yes, if he's not arrested by accident and hanged. It would be very difficult being his widow."

"When did you become such a doom-and-gloom?"

"Since…always!" Was this true? She had spoken the words out loud. "Doomed to be tall, homely and always alone."

Melinda stood, wobbling for balance on her crutch.

"Rebecca Louise Lane! If I hear you say such a thing again, I'm going to bean you over the head with this!" She waved the crutch madly in the air. "You are beautiful…but you are just too damn stubborn to believe it."

Melinda covered her mouth. Her eyes went wide as saucers. This was the first time her cousin had used profanity.

"I'm going back to the house before you and your stubborn, ridiculous and very wrong vision of yourself make me someone Mama would be ashamed of…more than she already is."

"I'll walk with you," Rebecca said, worried that the crutch might catch uneven ground and trip Melinda up.

"I can make it on my own, Miss Blind to the Truth. I don't even need this thing anymore. I only use it to squash beetles and flip away snakes." Melinda pushed her way out of the barn. "And for pity's sake, stand up tall!"

Rebecca watched while her cousin made the long walk toward the house. Actually, Melinda was doing much better these days, but Lantree had not given her leave yet to abandon the crutch.

She was nearly ready to run after Melinda when Lantree strode around the corner of the bunkhouse.

He spotted Melinda, hurried forward and helped her back to the house. She spoke animatedly to him then glanced back to stab her with a frown.

When they reached the stairs, Lantree slipped his strong, supportive arm about Melinda's tiny waist. He dipped his head down, speaking close to her ear while he helped her up.

Upon reaching the top he turned, looking at Rebecca through the dimming light of early evening. He was frowning and, she thought, none too happy.

Let him be angry if he wanted to. It was a far better state than the utterly brokenhearted one she was in.

She closed the barn door, then flung herself down on the hay bale and said, "One, no man will ever tell me what..."

Then she wept.

* * *

Supper had come and gone. Rebecca had not returned from the barn.

Lantree stood on the porch of the main house, leaning against the post and looking down the slope, past the paddock. There was no light leaking under the barn door, which meant she had not even bothered to light a lantern.

A sad, very lonely melody drifted toward the house. Guess with her talent, she didn't need light to guide her fingers.

She'd told him that Catherine Rose's spirit was with her. The first time she'd said that he'd been a scoffer…but not anymore. Catherine's soul came across in every note Rebecca drew from the instrument. He'd never heard the violin played with such beauty.

Right now she must be feeling desolate. Hell and damn, so was he.

Without a moon, the night was dark as pitch. In the distance he heard a wildcat screech. Closer in, bears would be silently prowling the night for food.

Lantree ground his boot heel on the porch in frustration.

Over the past few weeks, he'd given Rebecca

space, time to work things out in her head. A man like him came with a load of problems.

But since his conversation with Melinda after dinner, he understood much more than he had. Rebecca's feeling of being the ugly duckling went much deeper than her aunt's treatment of her, and of growing up compared to Melinda most of her life.

Rebecca's vision of herself had more to do with her mother's desertion…and her father's.

The image he had in his mind of a sweet little girl being left on her aunt's front porch without a backward glance broke his heart.

If Eunice had been a more sensitive person, she might have nurtured Rebecca, not put the blame that her sister deserved on an innocent child. Until she arrived at the ranch, the only one who had shown Rebecca unconditional love had been Melinda.

He could only imagine what it had felt like for Rebecca, feeling as she did about herself, to be in the constant company of her cousin, a woman who drew comments of admiration wherever she went.

Hell and damn! That kind of thinking was going to end tonight. He was finished with this waiting game. Snatching his rifle from the rack beside the front door he stomped down the porch steps two at a time.

He was going to claim his wife.

Glancing left and right he searched the shadows for any sign of a night prowler, be it two- or four-legged. The only thing shuffling in the shadows was the wind bending the treetops and twirling the dirt about his boots.

The barn door squealed when he flung it open. The music stopped. He heard a rustle in the straw pile in the far corner of the barn. Didn't sound like a mouse.

"Rebecca Walker, I've come to bring you home!"

Heavy boot falls pounded the hard packed floor of the barn. Even in the dark they did not slow down or stumble, but came toward her like an arrow to a target.

Lantree crouched beside her then scooped her up.

"Put me down," she demanded but he strode back the way he had come, carrying her weight without seeming the slightest bit winded. "You can't just haul me about like…like—"

Well, clearly he could. And to be honest,

while it made her feel powerless, it was in a curiously pleasant way.

"I demand that you set me free!" She flailed her legs and shoved his chest knowing very well that he was not going to even loosen his grip. In her heart of hearts, she knew that she did not want him to.

Outside, the wind had begun to howl over and under the barn eaves. Great gusts tore at the treetops and across the ground.

He hauled her past the big house. From the parlor window she saw Grandfather with his arm slung about Melinda's shoulder. Why, the pair of them were grinning like loons!

Without losing his grip on her, Lantree opened the front door of the cabin and swept inside.

All of a sudden it hit her, how much she had missed her cozy home and how very much she had missed sharing it with Lantree.

Still, she could hardly steal Melinda's beloved.

"You can't keep me here against my will, Lantree Walker."

"Give me a minute," he said, setting her on the floor after a long, slow slide down his body. "And it won't be against your will."

He set his rifle aside without letting go of her,

then he cupped her face in his hands, stroking her cheeks with his thumbs.

Dipping his head, he kissed her. She gave herself over to it for a moment but Melinda's face flashed in her mind and she turned her head to the side.

"This is not right." She tried to yank away but he only tugged her in tighter, so tight that she felt the heavy thud of his heart.

"You are my wife. Nothing could be more right if it's what you want, Becca."

"What I want is for you and Melinda to be happy…together."

"Me and Melinda?" His brows arched. "Is that what's made you so standoffish? There's a man for your cousin, but he isn't me."

"But she's in love with you! I saw the exact second it happened. It was the very first time she looked at you."

"I won't deny that Melinda loves me, she told me so not more than an hour ago."

Oh, why could the cabin floor not open up and swallow her whole? To suspect something was ever so much easier than hearing the truth spoken out loud.

"Then why have you dragged me here?"

"I'll quote the exact conversation we had.

'You need to do something about Rebecca,' Melinda said. 'Would if I damn well knew what,' from me. Then she says, 'Think about it. My cousin believes I'm in love with you because the first time I saw you I fell into a magnificent crush, because who wouldn't... Well, Becca noticed and now she believes that I love you, and because she thinks so harshly of herself, she believes that you must be madly in love with me, too.' I was dumbfounded, so she said, 'Go set my fool cousin straight.' I said, 'Hell and damn!' Then she said, 'It is true that I love you, but it's because you love my Becca so very much.'"

He took a long breath, clearly waiting for her reaction.

"By the saints!" Every word that he quoted would have been exactly what Melinda would say. But— "It makes no sense. How could you not be in love with Melinda? She's an exceptional beauty, kind and funny and—and everyone loves her."

"Because I love you!"

Humph! Why did he look so annoyed about it?

"Once and for all I am going to put an end to this ugly duckling nonsense," he said.

"Well, they do say beauty is in the eye of the beholder, so you might be—"

He took her roughly, but not unpleasantly, by the wrist and pulled her behind him into the bedroom. There was a long glass mirror in the corner and he positioned her in front of it then lit the lamp on the bedside table. A soft glow shimmered off their reflections. Outside, the wind slammed against the house.

"Tell me what you see…and be honest, not so stubborn that you'll deny the truth just to be right in your own mind."

"I see an exceptionally handsome Viking of a man standing behind me. He looks peeved about just having declared his love, though."

"Not peeved." He kissed her temple. "Only determined to make you take off those blinders and see the incredible woman that I see."

"You and my cousin, both of you cut from the same cloth. Really, Lantree, I do have eyes in my head."

He placed his fingers on her waist. The span of his hands was so large that it nearly circled it.

"I aim to make you see yourself through my eyes. I challenge you to hold your tongue while I do."

He lifted one hand from her waist to trace the curve of her cheekbone.

"Harsh, angular," she muttered.

"Hush." He nipped her ear. A delicious chill washed over her. "A goddess would envy them.

"Nicely arched brows," he said, tracing the shape of them, one by one. "Pretty eyes, full of intelligence and humor. They shine with the joy of being alive. That's something you would not be able to see on your own. Don't you know that whenever you smile at someone it lights up their day?"

She held her tongue. It was true that she had always appreciated the shape of her brows.

"Lips made for kissing." He looked at them for a moment in the glass, his gaze heating up as he did.

"A long slender neck, so graceful and..." His fingers dipped to her collar... He opened a button. Behind her she felt his breath quicken when he traced the hollow of her throat with his thumb. "Attached to the most exquisitely formed female body I have ever seen."

She snapped her head around. "You've never seen my female body!"

"Twice." A wide grin spread his mouth. "The first time barely counted since I was tending your wounds and trying to remain professional. I will admit, it did take some effort. But the next time there was water glistening all over you and I enjoyed that very much."

"You mean at camp? You spied on my bath?"

"By accident. Look back at the mirror." He turned her chin so that she could do nothing else.

"It's time, Becca."

One by one he opened the buttons of her dress, all the way down to the waist. He drew her arms out of the sleeves, then pressed the body of the gown past her hips. It billowed down, making a blue puddle at her feet.

"I love you. You will be mine."

The heat of his gaze and the warmth of his breath on her ear told her this was true. That he meant to make her his wife in every way, just as he had promised that night by the pond.

She wanted that, too. But try as he might, he would not make her believe that she was pretty. She was plain. A fact was a fact.

She'd been looking at the mirror, so she should have noticed that he'd loosened the pink ribbon holding her underclothes together. However, what she had been watching were the changing expressions flitting across his face. She hadn't noticed that he had removed the rest of her clothing until she felt cool air brushing her skin.

To her astonishment, she was standing before

him naked…for the third time. The only thing protecting her modesty was the fall of thick hair covering her chest, and her splayed hands where she crossed them over the junction of her thighs.

Heat flared from her face. Her throat, normally as pale as milk, pulsed with red splotches.

Long fingers, tanned and calloused, touched one red spot, then another. Slowly, he drew the hair away from one side of her neck and tucked it behind her shoulder, fully revealing her left breast. He suckled her skin where her neck curved into her shoulder.

He drew the hair back from her right side, baring her, then kissing her throat on that side. She felt the scrape of flannel against her back, the rub of denim on her bottom and thighs.

"Tell me what you see," he murmured. The cool circle of moisture where his mouth had been made her shiver.

"Can't…speak…just now," she panted. How could he expect her to when she could barely draw a breath or form a thought?

"Here's what I see…pale and lovely breasts, tipped by sweet brown nipples blushed with pink."

Oh, by the saints, her legs were trembling. How long would she be able to stand here watching him watch her…staring wide-eyed while he cupped her breasts, one in each large hand.

Clearly, Lantree Walker knew what to do with the female body. He watched in the mirror while her nipples tightened. Then he kneaded, stroked, cupped and tugged until she gasped. Whatever magic he was laving on her made her want to behave in a most unladylike way. It was all she could do to press her knees together.

"Look at yourself, Becca. Can you see yourself through my eyes yet?"

"Umm—" It was a moan more than an answer, but he was beginning to make his point. She wanted to stretch like a cat and purr. She could not recall a cat that was not confident in its beauty.

He took her hands, drew them apart, one by one.

"Let me tell you then." His voice had grown hoarse. "I see my beautiful wife, with curvy hips and long shapely thighs. Even your feet…those high arches and slender toes are all woman."

Those very toes gripped the floor without even feeling it. Womanly feet? By the saints! He might be getting carried away and to be impeccably honest, she did not mind.

"Here's the truth, love. You're mistaken in

thinking beauty comes from being petite and delicate. You, with your long graceful limbs, are sumptuous…radiant. You have more beauty inside your soul than I've ever seen.

"I know that your mother left you, your father did, too, and that made you, an innocent child, think lowly of yourself. Listen to me. Let this sink down into your soul…I will never leave you. You are everything to me, Becca."

Watching his face in the mirror, seeing that he meant it, her heart understood. He loved her and that made her beautiful.

For the first time in her life, she felt pretty. When she had expected to feel ill-favored standing naked before this exceptionally virile man, she did not.

Dizzy…she felt so light… No, it was more like heavy…drugged.

Lantree supported her weight with one muscled arm about her waist. She felt the scrape of denim on her bottom. His suntanned skin made hers look pale…and, she had to admit, delicate.

His free hand touched her belly, rubbing gently and trailing downward, lower and lower until— *Oh…oh, my.*

With two fingers, he gently spread her feminine folds. She saw a flash of swollen pink, then it was hidden by his fingers as they stroked her.

"You are the loveliest woman I've ever seen. Do you believe it yet?"

"Yes." She closed her eyes because the sensations he drew from her were so delightfully intense.

"Open your eyes, Becca. I want you to see what I see."

She sought his eyes in the mirror, held his gaze while she shattered.

Chapter Fourteen

Taking her by the shoulders, Lantree turned Rebecca away from the mirror and wrapped her in an embrace. The scent of her on his fingers made him want to howl like a beast, jump upon her and claim her.

But he was not a beast so he held her tenderly, stroking her back and murmuring in her ear that he loved her.

He squeezed her bottom cheeks, both of them in one big hand, while with the other hand he cradled the back of her head. He kissed her long and hard...tasted her with slow seduction.

Leaves slapped the windows, branches creaked in trees, but inside the lamp glowed softly, making the cabin a refuge.

"Come, love," he whispered in her ear while guiding her backward.

The backs of her knees butted the bed. She

tumbled down, her breasts jiggling as she settled into the give of the mattress.

"But I want to see you undress in front of the mirror," she said.

"You be my mirror."

Very slowly, he yanked his shirt from his pants then tossed it on the floor.

"Don't dawdle," she chided. "You've made me feel all twitchy inside."

"That's all part of the pleasure."

She flung her arms wide across the mattress. "Don't tell me I've married a cruel man."

Her words might sound cross, if breathless, but she gazed up at him, her lids half-lowered, her expression soft and dreamy.

"You've married a grateful man."

Finally naked, he stretched his length on top of her. He knew he was solid, heavy as stone, but not a flicker of unease crossed her expression.

He'd told her he was grateful, but it went so much deeper than that. At last here was a woman he could get lost in. Go with her into passion, to the place where they would become lost to everything, except to each other.

Before he could do that, though, there was one thing—

"Rebecca, I want you, you know I do, but the

way we were married, you never had a choice. What I want to know is, do you choose me now? Not the now as in right now, but do you choose me…for always? Do you want this marriage?"

"I take you, Lantree Boone Walker to be my lawfully wedded husband, to have and to hold."

She touched the side of his face with a delicate stroke.

He lifted up on his elbows to better see her expression. She smiled, her eyes moist, shining in the lamplight.

"From this day forward," he answered. "Forsaking all others."

"For better or for worse, until death do us part… You may kiss your bride…or do anything else you have in mind."

"Were you a good student in school, Mrs. Walker?"

"I was dedicated to my studies."

"Let's get down to lessons, shall we?"

"I love you, Lantree."

He kissed the tender flesh between her breasts so that he could feel her heartbeat under his mouth.

"I aim to make you so happy that you never regret it," he whispered.

Sweet cream could not be more delectable

than the smooth glide of her skin under his tongue. A breeze on a sweltering summer night could not be more sultry than her sigh of surrender against his ear.

"I'm going to learn what you taste like, Becca, every line, dent and fold of you."

"What fold?" The breath hitched in her lungs. Clearly she was shocked, but there was no mistaking the curiosity in her voice.

"The one that got you blushing."

"Do people—"

Her question ended abruptly when he eased downward and spread her thighs.

"The blessed ones do," he answered.

Some thoughts were in his mind, but with the female scent of her so close, words dried up.

He tasted her then became lost in sensation. Sex had never been like this before.

But God had granted him a perfect mate. She was his match. He didn't mean only her amazing body, but also her sweet, bold and independent soul.

Glancing up, he saw that Rebecca was as consumed as he was. Even though this was her first time, she did not show apprehension. She gazed back at him with all the fever he felt burning inside him.

He reached up to cup, to fondle her breasts, then slid up her belly and her ribs with slow hot kisses.

Her hips lifted under his with a shy thrust. She clutched his shoulders.

He nudged her with his erection, hesitant… wondering if with the moment upon them she might tense up…perhaps withdraw from him.

Then, he felt her fingers upon him, inviting him into her body…and into the rest of her life.

Coming into her slowly, he felt the world fall into place about him. Tender flesh clenched about him and he thrust faster rushing headlong to where there was only Becca, the scent of her and the sound of her sighs…hurtling to that place where the harshness of the world fell away and left perfect peace in its place.

At noon, Lantree drew Rebecca into the barn after him and pulled the door closed against the wind, which had only intensified during the morning hours.

Somehow he hadn't noticed it so much last night. His wife had occupied his full attention. She was every bit of the woman that he had daydreamed about…her inner fire and her easy laugh…her soft sigh as he penetrated her.

Hell and damn, he'd forgotten that the rest of the world existed until Rebecca had announced that she was hungry.

So was he, now that he looked beyond the bed. If he was hungry, the stock must be, as well.

He'd promised his wife that he would return quickly, but Rebecca had insisted on coming with him.

Now that he glanced about the barn, some interesting possibilities occurred to him.

With the wind as strong as it was, no one would be likely to venture outside.

Rebecca stared at the fresh pile of straw in one of the stalls. She glanced up at him with a grin.

"I'll fetch a blanket from the tack room."

He hurried into the back room, lifted the blanket from the shelf, then met Rebecca in the stall. He spread the red wool over the straw.

"Wait here while I feed the animals."

"I could help," she said.

"I reckon seeing you waiting for me will set fire to my heels."

Rebecca was not idle in her waiting. Taking off her shoes, she wriggled her lovely long toes at him. Next she plucked off her garters, rolled down her stockings and tossed them.

By the time she had opened the front of her

dress and bared her chemise, he had finished the feeding.

With a whoop and a leap, he landed in the straw beside her. She laughed and he whipped her beneath him, rucking up her skirt as he did.

A sudden gust of air blew his hair and rippled the back of his shirt.

"Boone Walker, stand up slow and easy," a voice, deep as a bear's growl, ordered. "Back away from the woman with your hands in the air."

Hell! Hell! Hell and damn! Sheriff Johnson stood in the doorway of the barn with his rifle across his chest and his long beard being tossed by the wind.

Standing beside him, the mayor of Coulson stared open-mouthed at Rebecca, who was quickly buttoning her dress. He could only take pride in the fact that her fingers were not trembling.

He stood up. A second later Rebecca was standing beside him, holding his hand.

"You've made a mistake. This is not Boone Walker," she pointed out. "This is Lantree Walker...Boone's twin brother."

"So he says," Smothers said, his voice a snarl.

"Got any proof of that?" Johnson asked, pointing his rifle barrel at the ground then leaning on the butt.

"I have proof," came a small voice from behind the sheriff and Smothers.

Both men spun about in surprise.

Lantree stifled a curse, seeing Melinda leaning on her crutch, her skirt blown about in the wind and tears dampening her pretty blue eyes.

With a great sigh she tried to close the barn door but it fought her.

"Sheriff Johnson?" She appealed to him with an irresistible pout of moist, pink lips.

He couldn't imagine the man who could resist being Melinda's champion.

Then again, judging by the scowl on Smothers's face, he reckoned he'd just found that man.

Johnson closed the door and was treated to Melinda's grateful smile.

"What's your proof, young woman?" The sheriff must have only been half-smitten with her because his voice still sounded full of gravel.

"Why, I'm married to Boone Walker." She blinked wide. "I do know the difference between the men…most of the time."

"She's lying!" The breath exploded from Smothers with a snort. He turned an unhealthy color.

"Would this be a time you know the difference, Mrs. Walker?"

"Oh, indeed." Melinda stepped close to the shaggy bear of a lawman, lifted her shoulders in a shrug. She whispered, but loud enough to be heard by them all. "It's not difficult when they have their clothes on."

"Arrest this man!" Smothers sputtered.

Melinda nodded her head with vigor. "Arrest them both, I say…but sadly, Lantree Walker is not guilty of any crimes…crimes that might get him arrested, that is."

"Where is your husband, ma'am, if this is not him?"

"If I knew that I'd lead you to him myself."

Melinda stroked the tears from her eyes. Unbelievably, Lantree felt Rebecca tremble in repressed laughter.

He frowned down at her. This was a serious situation and she seemed to be amused by it. He couldn't help but wonder what kinds of trouble the girls had wriggled their way out of growing up.

He reckoned he ought to speak up for himself, but he wanted to know where this was leading.

"I'm afraid you gentlemen have come at a difficult time." Melinda looked at Rebecca.

"The very worst, I'm afraid," Rebecca agreed.

"I'm sorry to say," the sheriff said, "there rarely is a good time for an arrest."

"This would be an excellent time, if only a crime against society had been committed." Melinda took a step closer to Johnson. She laid her delicate fingers on the rough, gnarled skin of his hand. "But the crime has been against me and my cousin…and she's a newlywed."

"Don't listen to that harlot," Smothers said, but Johnson ignored him. "The three of them are in cahoots. Lock them all up, I say."

"If I am a harlot, it is not by my own choice." She cast a glare at Lantree that made him feel guilty of—something. And what that was, he feared he was about to find out.

Johnson was treated to a blush of rose-petal cheeks.

"As I said a moment ago, it's easy to tell them apart when they are clothed, but otherwise they look exactly alike. They even… And last night—"

"Last night!" Rebecca exclaimed, shoved Lantree in the chest then turned her stricken gaze upon her cousin. "You and I on the same night?"

All at once Melinda pushed past Smothers and the sheriff to embrace Rebecca.

"What if we've both conceived?" she wailed. "What will our children be?"

Melinda turned to Smothers. She swished her ruffled skirt toward him and let the tears slide down her cheeks unchecked. "Perhaps you know, Mr. Mayor, will they be siblings or cousins?"

"Bastards," he announced.

With a squeal, Melinda launched herself into Johnson's arms. His gun thumped to the barn floor. His arms came about her while she wept into his beard. He patted her back one time.

Lantree jumped, startled when Rebecca poked her finger at his nose.

"You low-down vile fornicator!"

Had the women rehearsed this skit before, or were they just that good?

"Arrest him, Mr. Johnson," Rebecca ordered. "I insist. If you think about it, they look the same. What difference would it make? You'd still have a criminal."

"I'm here to arrest a murderer, ma'am, not a fornicator. Until I get to the truth we'll all spend a cozy afternoon right here. I ain't in no mood to go back out into that devil of a wind, as it is."

All at once Smothers's expression shot back

and forth between Rebecca and Melinda. The cold calculation in his narrowed gaze turned every muscle in Lantree's body tense in anticipation of plowing the mayor into the barn wall.

"I imagine you want to find out the truth without the ladies present," he said, suddenly and deceitfully, appearing the gentleman that his fancy clothing said he was. "I'll just escort them outside."

"Take me to Coulson, Johnson," Lantree said quietly while he held his hands out for cuffing. "I'll go easy as long as the mayor goes with us. You ought to know that there's bad blood between him and me. He's not here to help in an honest arrest. He's here to cause trouble and for no other reason."

Smothers focused his attention on Rebecca, some kind of wicked lust-revenge expression twisting his face. He could only hope that Johnson saw it, as well.

"I'll just slow you down," Smothers said. "I'll stay and protect the ladies from this *violent* weather while you make your way through the lies."

Smothers let the word violent cross his lips a little too slowly.

"You want a peaceful arrest, Sheriff, you'll leave here with the both of us."

Johnson looked him up and down, his gaze hard. By reputation, this was not a man to rile up.

Still, there was no doubt that Lantree was, at this moment, threatening violence. Hippocratic oath or not, he would do harm to Smothers before he would leave Becca and Melinda alone with him.

All of a sudden, Smothers reached for Rebecca's arm. Rebecca balled her fist and swung it at his face but missed. Melinda, shrieking in outrage, delivered her boot to Smothers's crotch.

He collapsed into a whining ball, rolling about on the barn floor.

Rebecca ran to Lantree and wrapped him in an embrace, even as Johnson handcuffed him.

"Get up, Smothers." Johnson poked him in the behind with the barrel of his shotgun. "I only got one pair of cuffs, but until we get to the truth of who is who, I've got my weapon pointed at your butt."

"Get back to the house, Becca." Lantree kissed her cheek. "I'll be home in a week."

"Or hanged." Smothers's words came out of him as a wheeze while he got to his feet.

"We'll escort you ladies to the house," Johnson said. "We'll be on our way once we know you are safe inside."

"By the saints, that will not do. I'm going," Rebecca insisted, as Lantree knew she would.

"Me, too!" Melinda decreed. Of course, he was not half-surprised at that, either.

"I can't keep you safe, not like this." He held up his cuffed hands. "If something happens to me, you've got to be here for your grandfather."

"Well…" Melinda sighed, apparently seeing the wisdom. "That makes some sense…but more than that, Becca, we can gather everyone we know and march on Coulson!"

"Truth in numbers." He could see Rebecca mulling this over.

"You ladies talking a mob?" the sheriff growled.

"Oh, certainly not!" Melinda cast a spellbinding glance at Johnson. "It's just that it's a wonderful thing to see justice done…the law at work to protect the innocent. I just know everyone in these parts would love to see their lawman at his very finest."

"Humph!" the lawman grunted, but under the dirty beard and bushy brows, Lantree thought he saw a blush of pleasure pulse in Liver-Eating Johnson's cheeks. "Let's go."

Chapter Fifteen

Rebecca stood on the porch of the big house watching Lantree until she could no longer see his long confident strides and the erect posture of his broad shoulders in the thick growth of trees beyond the house.

Lengthening shadows of midafternoon lashed across the flower beds in the wind. Branches creaked. Some splintered and crashed down, littering the yard.

It wasn't safe for him to be out in this blow. And to make things worse, the temperature was falling. He'd been taken from home without a coat or hat.

"I should take him a blanket. If I hurry—"

"Becca, you can't and you know it." Melinda looked up at her, her expression serious. "That wicked little man means you harm. You won't want Lantree to be using his efforts watching out for you when he needs to be figuring a way out of this mess."

"But I can't stand the thought of him being cold."

"As much as we want to, there are some things we can't do for a man." Melinda's expression brightened again. "And there are some things that we can."

"March the neighbors?"

"Exactly. We'll send Jeeter to rally them as soon as the weather changes. With all those witnesses to vouch for his identity, your man will be free in five minutes."

"I dread going inside and telling Grandfather what has happened." Rebecca bit her bottom lip, agitation making her feel like a butterfly trapped in a mason jar. "I'd rather cut out my tongue."

"I know that's just creative speech, but let's go do some slicing and get this over with."

Inside, the house was quiet, which for this time of day wasn't so odd, but something felt off. The quiet was different.

Normally the clink of pots would announce that Barstow had begun to prepare dinner. He would be speaking with Kiwi Clyde about the menu.

The bird was on his perch, not in the kitchen.

"Something's wrong," she said even though Melinda would have already noticed.

"The rifles beside the door are gone. So are the ones over the fireplace."

"Do you think they've gone after Lantree?" She felt suddenly sick. Agitated men and guns could easily end in bloodshed.

"We'd have noticed. Unless they went another way and plan to get ahead of Johnson." Melinda shook her head. "But I don't think so. The timing doesn't seem right to me. How could they have discovered the trouble, organized a plan, got away so quickly? Lantree's only been gone twenty minutes."

"When you came out of the house everything was normal?"

"Grandfather was napping in his chair, Barstow was kissing Kiwi Clyde. Jeeter was... Oh, my, he was pounding up the steps shouting something as I was going out. I paid him no attention because he's always in a high spirit over something, and I'd just seen the sheriff and the mayor go into the barn and I knew you and Lantree had gone into the barn and knew that you wouldn't be, um, prepared for visitors."

Melinda screwed up her face in her thinking expression. Rebecca knew from experience that the more compressed her cousin's lips and the more lines crinkling the corners of her eyes, the harder she was thinking.

Luckily Melinda had an excellent memory. Just as soon as the line creeping up her forehead reached her hairline, she would recall what Jeeter had been shouting.

"Rustlers!" she exclaimed, her blue eyes popping wide open.

"Cattle or trees?" It made a difference.

"Trees…near the river and not far from home." Melinda glanced about in frustration. "The guns are gone. How are we to help?"

"We don't know how to shoot anyway."

"We wouldn't have to shoot, only look like we meant to. They wouldn't know that we're not a pair of Annie Oakleys."

By the saints! They didn't need Annie when they had Medusa.

"How would you feel about wearing snakes in your hair?"

"Dead or alive?"

"There are a bunch of skinned rattlers hanging on the wall in the tack room in the barn. I'll meet you there. I'm going to put on a brown dress and grab my violin."

"You have a brown dress?"

"I do and it is practical on occasion," she called, dashing out of the house. She leaped over a fallen log then glanced back at Melinda, who was already hobbling toward the barn. "Be careful!"

Lantree felt the grit of a two-hour hike coating his teeth. He swallowed, but the cursed wind had dried out the inside of his mouth. Unless it was urgent, he refrained from speaking.

The same could not be said of Smothers, who had not ceased to complain about everything from leaving the horses such a distance from the ranch, to the rip in the knee of his suit, to the injustice of Johnson confiscating his weapon… and that he was tired.

That last did seem a concern. In Lantree's medical opinion, and he could only admit that for the first time in a while it did feel good to have one, the man did not look well.

"I gotta rest, Johnson," he panted. Maybe this was for show and maybe not. His high coloring said maybe it wasn't.

"If we stop every time you feel winded, Smothers, we won't make it back to Coulson before Christmas."

"By observing him," Lantree spoke up, "I'd

say his body is under some stress. Heart, lungs maybe, can't be sure just by looking, though."

"Never met a hardened killer that knows medicine," Johnson said.

"And you haven't now, either," Lantree replied then eased down on a rock beside a stream. "I became a doctor after the shooting involving my brother. And in the interest of truth, Sheriff, I was there when the killing happened. It was self-defense with a lying witness thrown into the mess."

"Where's your shingle, Doc?" Smothers said, his color improving now that he was sitting down. "Can't recall that you've treated a single person in Coulson."

It was true. Maybe he ought to have. For the first time in years he wondered if distancing himself from healing had been the right choice. While he'd been caring for ailing livestock, had he failed in his obligation to folks in need?

"I'm going to hunt up some grub for dinner. If either one of you move your asses a hair out of place I'll shoot you where you sit."

Lantree leaned against a tree, then slid down to sit with his knees bent. He anchored his cuffed hands about his knees and stared at Smothers.

"This arrest is about my wife?" he asked.

Smothers laughed, but it was an ugly sound. "About making her a widow, more to the point."

"Even with me out of the way, you'd never be able to handle her."

"I've found that women generally come to understand who is boss at the end of a balled-up fist. The giant would be no different."

"Just to make this clear, I won't let you even breathe on her."

"This time tomorrow I'll be doing a whole lot more than breathing on her, and you won't be able to do spit about it."

"I'll do spit and more. Count on it."

"Not after you've been shot to death trying to escape."

"I'm keeping my butt planted right here."

"Only because you don't know the trouble happening at the ranch as we speak. Pretty clever how I got you out of the way."

His stomach lurched then hit bottom.

"You stunned to silence, or just too yellow to ask what's happening?"

"I reckon you are trying to take what isn't yours, and just now I'm studying a way to keep you from doing it. Might be a sight easier if you tell me what you think is happening at the ranch."

"I know what's going on. I made the plan, hired the men. They're cutting prime trees near the river, to rile the old man as much as anything. Once all is said and done, I'll decimate every damn hunk of wood on the place. But all I need for today is to get rid of you and old man Moreland."

"You're in bad health, Smothers. I wasn't making that up about your heart and lungs. What are you going to do with all that property when you're dead? Seems to me that it will go right back to Rebecca and you will have gained nothing."

A gunshot echoed from close by. After a moment, footsteps crunched over twigs that the wind had shaken loose from the trees.

Smothers stared him down and he stared back. One of them would be dead before nightfall and they both knew it.

Johnson, being pushed from behind by a gust, appeared in the clearing carrying a pair of rabbits. One shot, two rabbits? The man must be as deadly a shot as his reputation said.

"Been sitting here, just like you said to," Smothers declared. "Couldn't say it was comfortable though, being left here without my weapon in the company of a known killer."

"Ain't nothin' going to be known until after the trial." Johnson turned his back and set the rabbits on a flat rock. Squatting, he took out his knife to begin the butchering. "Can't say this man here is any more guilty of a crime than you are until the judge and jury have their say."

Johnson had set his shotgun aside to gut the rabbits. Smothers shot it a swift, sidelong glance.

As quick as a viper, Smothers ran across the clearing and snatched it up.

Lantree shouted.

Johnson spun about, flung the butcher knife, dripping red with rabbit blood, and impaled Smothers in the neck.

He fell face-first, his arms twitching.

"Unlock my hands!" Lantree shouted at the cursing lawman. "Before he bleeds to death."

"Got my piece on you," Johnson said, but he hurried to unlock the cuffs.

Lantree turned Smothers over, careful to keep the knife from shifting and doing more harm than had already been done.

"Mortal wound," Johnson pronounced, gazing down over his shoulder. "Seen my share of those."

And delivered his fair share, as well, so the stories went.

"Put some pressure here, beside the knife," Lantree said.

He couldn't make sense of why he was trying to save this man's life since Johnson was probably right about it being a mortal wound. And there was no reason he should want Smothers to live except that he had taken an oath.

An oath that he had ignored for a very long time.

While the sheriff applied pressure, Lantree carefully removed the blade. Even if Smothers did survive the cut, he doubted the man's heart could take the stress of the loss of blood.

Pressing his fingers to the mayor's neck, he felt for a pulse.

"It's weak, but keep on pressing like you are and see if he stabilizes."

"Can't figure why you'd want him to. Seems to me he was out to do you harm."

"There is that part of me that would be relieved to see him die. But hell and damn, man, I'm a doctor. I've had my fill of watching folks die."

"Fill or not, this one's got the color of death on him. You're wasting your time, Walker."

He nodded because he knew it to be true, but…

The pulse under his fingertips stuttered, stopped.

With a nod he sat back and gripped his thighs.

Johnson stared at him for a long time. Weighing his fate in the balance, no doubt.

"You're free to go, Dr. Walker." Johnson extended a handshake. "Your brother's still as wanted as ever, even though I might believe you about the shooting being unintended."

"I'll need a horse. Smothers hired men to attack my family. Said they were at the ranch now."

He needed to be home. Even a fast ride might not be enough to get him to Moreland Ranch in time.

"Let's go," Johnson said, setting off into the woods at a run.

"I've got to say, cousin, you do look frightening."

"Repulsive…and wonderful all rolled into one." Melinda fluffed the horror on her head, preening.

Rebecca reached out to touch one of the dozen snakes that she had weaved into Melinda's hair then secured into a wicked halo with wire.

"What ghoulish piece will you play?"

"I expect that Chopin's funeral march ought to send them running for home."

"It might send me running for home."

Even though the wind had begun to settle, hefty gusts still came out of nowhere to shake the trees and brush.

Melinda walked close beside Rebecca, listening for angry shouts or gunfire.

In the end it was seeing a treetop toppling in the distance that showed them where they needed to be.

Luckily, the distance was not far, not even a mile. Looking down from the top of a hill, they saw several trees littering the ground.

Melinda gripped her arm and eased down to kneel behind the fallen trunk. She laid her crutch in the dirt beside her.

Less than a hundred yards down the embankment men had lit a campfire for the evening. The conversation was loud and the jokes not meant for feminine ears.

"With all the noise they're making, I don't think they care if they get caught," Melinda whispered. "In my opinion this whole tree-napping is not for wood. It's a trap, Becca, and it's you they want. Doesn't it seem an odd coincidence that your husband was carted off at the same time the tree cutting started? That Smothers fellow wanted him away from here."

It did make sense. No genuine tree-napper would cut so close to the house.

"If it is me they want, they know what bait to use. Look over there a ways… It's Grandfather, Jeeter and Tom all sitting on a log."

"Tied up." Melinda squinted her eyes. "Oh, and look! They're making Barstow cook…something. What is it, do you think?"

She shook her head. Barstow disdained cooking outside over an open flame. "Whatever it is, it's going to taste like mud."

"How many men do you see?" Melinda asked.

The light was growing dim and the figures were moving so it was hard to tell.

"Four," she said at last. "No…no, it's five."

"Five men against the ghost of Catherine Moreland?" Melinda shrugged and arched one brow. "I'd feel sorry for them if they weren't such greedy perverts."

"How is your leg? I'm sure you've walked too long on it."

"A twinge now and again, but really, it's fine… Oh, no!"

"'Oh, no'? What?"

"Two more men have come and they are pointing weapons at our men."

"Mike and Dimwit, unless I miss my guess." The light was growing dim but she was sure it was them.

"You rarely do...Becca, do you think we should go home?"

"You know I won't leave Grandfather a prisoner, especially if I'm the one they are waiting for. Now with Mike here, I'm sure you're right about this whole situation."

"You know what I think, Becca?"

"What?"

"It's not just the two of us behind this log... I think Catherine Rose is here, too."

That was a comfort. While they might frighten the wits out of the men below with Grandmother's ghost, she was greatly relieved to have her spirit accompanying them.

"We'll wait a few more minutes, until it's full dark and the moon begins to rise."

"And until they eat whatever vile feast Barstow has prepared. If he hasn't put something in it to make them vomit, I'll be astonished."

"You said something once, and you were right, Melinda. It was when you said that if you

stayed in Kansas City you would be stifled…
I'm so glad you came."

"Maybe one day I'll find my daydream man,
just like you did."

All of a sudden her heart ached. Where was
Lantree? Was he safe? The sooner this mess
below was straightened out, the sooner they
could gather the neighbors and bring him home.

"There it is," Rebecca announced when the
moon, a big fat yellow ball, cleared the horizon.

"Time to bring our men home."

Rebecca removed her violin from its case then
began to descend the hill.

"Whatever you do," she told Melinda, "stay
away from Mike, the fat one with the big nose.
He's trouble in the worst way and he won't be
afraid of Catherine Rose."

"What's this slop?" a man bellowed from
below. "It tastes like—"

All of a sudden the fellow covered his mouth
and dashed into the woods.

"By George, what did he expect?"

Rebecca looked at her cousin and instead
found herself staring into the eye of a dead
snake, but it didn't look dead because moonlight shone on its empty eye socket.

Even she was unnerved by the sight.

When they had snuck within fifty feet of the campfire, they hid behind a dense bush.

"I'll play for thirty seconds and then you rise from the foliage. When we've caught their attention we'll quit for a time then reappear over there."

Rebecca drew the bow across the strings of her violin. The mournful melody suffused the campsite. The hair rose on her arms when what could only be described as a warm breath caressed her fingers.

Through a thin spot in the foliage, she saw her grandfather lift his head and glance about. He nudged Jeeter in the side with his elbow. Jeeter poked Tom.

Melinda rose from the weeds, lifted her arms and swayed.

"It's her!" Dimwit screeched. "Ain't no amount of money Smothers can pay me to make it worth annoying a banshee. Let her keep her trees. I'm heading for home."

Melinda slowly glided back into the bush.

"You yellow-bellied coward!" Mike shouted at Dimwit's retreating figure. "I'll shoot you where you stand."

This set-to gave her and Melinda the cover they needed to track to the other side of the camp and crouch behind a fallen log. The cuts from the axes left gouges in the wood. Sap oozed from the wounds, filling the air with the scent of resin.

An odd sensation tingled her fingertips…irritation, she was sure of it. What could this be but Catherine Rose expressing her anger over her trees?

By George, it did not seem logical or sane, but there it was nonetheless.

"Two of them are gone," Rebecca said. "Only five more, but one of them is Mike."

"Strike up those strings, Becca."

The funeral march settled over the campsite, dark, oppressive and echoing among the trees so that it was difficult for the criminals to know exactly were it came from…until Medusa rose up behind them and screeched.

They hadn't discussed the screech, but it sent two more men running for the woods.

Melinda dragged her crutch behind her as they took the moment of confusion to duck behind a large shrub twenty feet away from Grandfather, Jeeter and Tom.

Barstow also took that moment to free Grandfather.

Once again, Mr. Chopin's morbid tune sent two more men into the dark woods. A wildcat's cry cut the night but the threat didn't send any of the men back to camp.

By the saints, they would not be back, and that left only Mike. Mike and his gun, which he had shoved against Grandfather's ribs.

Jeeter shouted profanity...then Tom shouted it louder. Barstow lifted a kettle of boiling water but set it down again, probably realizing that if he tossed it on Mike, it would burn Grandfather, as well.

"I know you ain't no spook, lady. Get on out here before I plug the old man."

Hell and damn! Lantree had held out a slight hope that Rebecca had remained safely at home. Until he'd heard the dirge, beautifully played, but a dirge nonetheless.

The hair-raising screech that followed had been Melinda's.

He'd raced the horse past a man vomiting in the bushes then another fleeing in white-faced fear.

Johnson had stopped a short distance back to arrest the first man they came across crashing through the brush. Lantree thought it was Dimwit, but didn't slow enough to find out for sure.

When he hit the rise of the hill, he went cold to the bone. The scene below was dire, shattering.

The full moon cast long blowing shadows of trees across the ground. The campfire's snapping flames were seven feet tall and made the faces within its glow look demonic.

One face needed no help with that. Snakes grew out of Melinda's hair.

He registered everything while he charged his mount down the hillside.

Mike pointing a gun at Rebecca. His face, by campfire, looking contorted…evil. Melinda standing beside Rebecca brandishing her crutch, as though she thought it might deflect a bullet.

Hershal only ten feet from his granddaughter, cussing and shouting.

Jeeter and Tom flanking him with their hands bound. Behind them Barstow working to loosen the bonds.

Hell and damn, he needed his weapon, but all he had was a pair of fists feeling like they were on fire.

Without slowing the horse, he tumbled off, rolled, then came to his feet in front of Rebecca and Melinda.

He spread his arms. "Put your gun down."

That made Mike laugh so hard that he doubled over.

"Didn't expect to see you here," he guffawed.

"Your boss is dead," Lantree said in case it would make a difference.

"No need to bring him your wife alive then, is there?" The laughter left Mike in a hurry. "You kill him?"

No one spoke.

Tree branches scratching against each other was the only sound until...

Faintly, so nearly inaudible that he would have doubted his senses, but for the shocked expressions on everyone's faces, came the lovely sigh of "Canon in D" whispering through the treetops. Just when everyone recognized it, the melody was gone, leaving only the trees scratching again.

"You owe me, Walker." Mike went on as though he hadn't heard a thing. Perhaps he hadn't. Could be that this was meant for loved ones. "Smothers was going to pay top dollar for her."

"That deal was dead before Smothers was."

"That so? Reckon I'll take my due in revenge... If I'm feeling kindly, I'll shoot your wife between the eyes. Come to think on it, though, I ain't. Step aside or I shoot you first."

Lantree spread his arms. "Never knew you to be insane, Mike, just a greedy bastard."

"You want to watch everyone here die before you do? Step aside or see how crazy I am."

The lunatic swung his pistol at Hershal. Lantree lunged at him and caught a pant leg.

Two shots exploded at the same time. Mike's head jerked backward. He crumpled, dead arms and legs collapsing.

Hershal grabbed his chest, looking stunned to see blood seeping past his fingers.

A figure appeared behind the clearing smoke of a shotgun…Johnson.

Behind Lantree Rebecca screamed.

The wind moved out but the rain moved in. Lamps from all over the house had been brought to the dining room where Hershal lay, his skin without color, blanched as white as the sheet that covered him from waist to toe.

Lantree touched his boss's forehead, smoothed back the hair from his brow and listened to the raindrops pelting the windows.

From wild wind to a gully washer of rain, this was not an easy land. Easy to love, though. He and Hershal had that in common…in common with everyone on Moreland Ranch.

"Hey, old man, you got a lot to live for," he

said quietly. "Everyone's in the parlor praying for you."

He took a breath and wished they were anywhere but in this situation.

While Lantree had abandoned his profession, he had not abandoned his instruments. They lay close at hand, a reach away, sterilized and ready to be used.

He'd gotten that far at least…the first step.

The question was, could he take the second? Could he cut into an old man's chest and dig for a bullet? An old man who meant everything to him…and to Rebecca.

He feared that he was destined to stand once more over a body, to tell the woman he loved that there was nothing he could do. This time would it be Rebecca's eyes that changed? Would he see the affection fade from them and resentment flash hot and angry?

"You know what to do, Lantree." Rebecca stood beside him, scrubbed as clean as the instruments on the table in front of her. "You haven't forgotten. Pick up the instrument that comes first, the rest will follow. Tell me what to do to help."

It wasn't a matter of forgetting the steps that needed to be taken, or how a scalpel felt in his hand. He remembered how bones and muscles knit together, how and where the blood flowed, the rhythms of life…and how to heal the things that went wrong.

He remembered it all.

It was other memories that held him back. The sounds of those in pain, the moans of the dying and the grief of the survivors.

And Eloise. Her strident voice publicly declaring him a failure.

But his Becca was not like Eloise in any way. Eloise had huddled in a corner, frightened, not even willing to look up from her weeping to wipe a fevered brow.

Rebecca looked at him with a confident smile, her eyes telling him she trusted him…that he could do this.

If he wanted Hershal to live, he needed to put Eloise away.

"Things are harder on the elderly," he told Rebecca. "Even if he makes it through the surgery, it will be a long hard recovery."

"You'll see him through it. I know you will."

He kissed her quickly. "I will."

Tears streamed down Rebecca's face when she pushed her way out of the dining room to give the news to those who had gathered in prayer.

"The bullet's out. Lantree is stitching him up

now. He stayed unconscious through the procedure…he still is."

"That's for the best," Melinda said past the hitch in her voice.

"I was shot once." Tom pointed to his rib. "Was out for days. Just got a little bitty scar to show for it, now."

"Didn't know you was shot!" Jeeter exclaimed.

By the saints! All of a sudden there was admiration glowing in the boy's eyes.

Lantree entered the dining room, wiping his hands on a white apron, wrinkled and smeared with blood.

He seemed different, even than he had when she'd left him a moment ago. This was something she felt more than she could see.

His grin was broad, his eyes alight with pleasure because things did point to Hershal's recovery.

But there was something else about him… Perhaps a part of himself that had been missing, had been restored.

"He's made it past the first and biggest hurdle," he announced. "I think he will recover."

"I don't think it," Barstow declared. "I know it."

"He's a tough old coot," Tom said.

"Too full of love for us all to not pull through," Melinda added.

"Anybody else wonder about the music?" Jeeter asked. "Was it maybe her calling him to come to her? Scared me out of my pants."

"Or—" the line between Melinda's eyes deepened while she thought "—maybe she was encouraging him to live."

"That must be it, since that's what he's going to do." Barstow stood up and clapped his hands. "Anybody hungry? I could eat a bear all of a sudden."

Johnson rose from the chair he had been sitting on for the past two hours, silent for the most part.

"So, in your professional opinion, I don't need to charge any of those fools tied up in the barn with murder?"

"Only attempted."

He nodded, his long beard sliding up and down. "I'll be on my way in the morning. See you all next time you're in Coulson, if the town's still got anybody in it by then."

With a tip of his hat, Johnson opened the front door and ducked out into the rain to spend the night in the barn with his captives.

"Jeeter…Tom, make up a stretcher, will you?

I'd like to get Hershal moved to his own bed before he comes to."

The scent of fresh rain blew in the doorway when they went outside.

"That was the longest two hours of my life," Melinda declared then used her crutch to ease down into one of the big stuffed chairs placed about the fireplace.

"You haven't been standing on it all this time, have you?"

"How's a body to pace fretfully while sitting in a chair?"

"You've stressed it tonight. Better let me have a look."

Lantree ran his hand over her shin. "There doesn't seem to be any damage. And…as fetching a look as it is, you might think about getting those snakes out of your hair."

"I don't know…some women wear bird nests in their hats. I might start a fashion."

Rebecca laughed, she couldn't help it. Maybe it was the relief of letting the stress go.

"I know what you are laughing at! What would Mama say if she could see me now?"

She nodded because she couldn't speak. When she was spent, she fell into the extra-large chair that Grandfather had given her and closed her eyes.

"Keep off that leg all day tomorrow."

"Yes, Dr. Walker." Melinda gave Lantree a radiant smile. "And someday when I have a baby, I want you to bring it into the world."

From where he still knelt beside Rebecca's chair, he glanced over at her. Their gazes locked.

Something shifted in her husband's eyes... It fell into place within him and she knew what it was.

She was married to a physician.

Epilogue

Nine months later

Rebecca placed her hands at the small of her back trying to rub away the ache.

By the saints, there wasn't much chance of rubbing away the early stages of labor.

Lantree had told her what to watch for, had quizzed her each morning before he rode out to check the herds for cows ready to give birth.

"At least you don't have to ride the hills looking for me," she had told him that morning with a playful nudge to his ribs.

And a very good thing, too. She'd had a mild cramp an hour earlier and now another one.

"Sit down, Rebecca," Grandfather said. "You'll wear the wax off the floor."

"You are going to spoil that bird with all the

peppermint sticks you give him. Last time I tried to give him a nut, he dropped it on the floor."

"I like spoiling him." Grandfather made kissing noises to Screech, who made kissing noises to his candy.

She stroked her belly. Her normally vigorous child had become quiet of late.

Her very own Dr. Walker had assured her that was often how it went in the hours before birth.

He would know. Since September he had delivered several babies for the settlers arriving by train.

The area was becoming more populated every day. Lantree had put out his shingle on a building that he rented behind the sawmill. He went downriver once a week to see to his patients. Generally, it was an overnight trip to get there, tend those in need and then get home again.

Even though Lantree had taken up his former career as a physician, he hadn't quit the one he had at Moreland Ranch.

The ranch was his now...and hers.

She had fallen in love with a cowboy and was glad that the earthy, dusty man had not really changed, only become the person he was meant to be.

A horse's hooves sounded in the yard. Rebecca

went to the window, disappointed to see that it was not her husband.

There had been another cramp and only twenty minutes had passed.

Melinda came down the stairs, looking fresh in a pale blue gown with a ruffled white apron.

She twirled about then stopped, letting the gown settle about her ankles.

"Well, what do you think, Becca? Do I look like a nurse?"

She didn't, not quite, but she would certainly cheer the patients up, if nothing else.

In the beginning, Rebecca had gone to the mill with Lantree to help him, but lately she had grown too cumbersome for that.

Melinda was going to take her place.

"I saw a man in the yard," her cousin said. "I'll find out what he wants."

"Take Grandfather with you," Rebecca called but Melinda's laughter echoed behind her and out onto the porch.

While the men who had been a danger to them were dead or in prison, that did not mean that everyone who rode up to the door in this remote area was good and kind.

A moment later Melinda escorted the fellow into the great room.

Slightly built, he held his hat in his hand and twisted it as though he were nervous.

"This is Mr. Stanley Smythe, come to see Lantree," Melinda said. "He assured me that he has nothing contagious."

Rebecca extended her hand in greeting at the same time as a stronger cramp threatened to double her up.

"Please have a seat, Mr. Smythe." She indicated one of the seven in front of the hearth. "Mr. Walker will be here shortly...I hope."

"You do?" Melinda eyed her sharply, looking back and forth between her belly and her face.

"Yes."

"I'll go fetch him."

"Let Jeeter do it. Maybe you can—" She took a long slow breath, the way Lantree had instructed her to do. Yes, that worked, much better now. "Get some refreshment for Mr. Smythe."

"I'll fetch Jeeter to fetch Lantree." Grandfather rose from his chair, only a bit slower than he had been at this time last year. Considering all he had been through he was doing remarkably well.

Rebecca eased down onto her chair. "Is there something I might help you with, sir?"

"No, this is business for Mr. Walker, and him alone."

"I see," she said, but she didn't and wanted to very badly.

Lantree needed to get home and in a hurry.

By George...here came another cramp, sooner and longer than the last one.

Melinda returned carrying a coffee mug in one hand and a plate with an assortment of pastries in the other.

Apparently, her cousin was also desperate to know Mr. Smythe's secretive business, because she sat down beside him and shot him a winsome smile while she handed him the treats, then the coffee.

"How very brave of you to come all the way here to deliver a message. You must have encountered at least a few wolves and bears." Melinda twirled a lock of hair about her finger, shivered her shoulders delicately. "Of course, you must be bursting to speak with Lantree... What a pity we do not know when he will return."

"Straightaway, I would imagine," Mr. Smythe said, shooting a glance at Rebecca then slanting a frown at Melinda.

That was odd. Very few men frowned at Melinda.

"Well, one never knows," Melinda continued, clearly undaunted by her inability to instantly enchant Mr. Smythe. No doubt she now considered him a challenge and was redoubling her efforts. "Perhaps you would like to rest from your travels upstairs. Mrs. Walker and I will be pleased to deliver your message."

"I don't doubt it."

Boots pounded the front stairs two at a time.

Lantree burst into the room breathing hard, a fine sheen of sweat glistening on his brow.

He greeted her with a long, slow kiss just like he always did. She melted into the scent of him, the press of his muscular body against hers... never mind that there was a stranger in the room.

"Lantree, this is Mr. Stanley Smythe. He—"

Lantree spared Mr. Smythe a brief nod, then ignored his diminutive presence completely. "Jeeter says it's your time."

"I think so...pretty sure, by George."

Lantree scooped her up and carried her upstairs to the room they planned to use for the birth and confinement. Not that she planned on being confined for long.

He set her gently on the bed, tossed up her

skirt then got down to the business of determining what was going on down below.

"Won't be long now, Mama," he announced with a grin. "I love you, Becca."

"I love you, too." She patted his cheek, rough with stubble. "Send up Melinda, then find out what it is that Mr. Smythe wants."

"Here, let's get you into something more comfortable."

Lantree reached into the wardrobe, shuffled clothes about, then drew out the gown she had planned to labor in.

"Lie down, I'll get your cousin." He set the gown beside her on the bed.

As soon as Lantree left the room she got up and began to walk from the bed to the window, the window to the bed. Her husband might be the doctor in the family but during her time at the ranch she'd seen a number of animals giving birth. She had rarely noticed them lying down during labor.

Melinda hurried into the room with an armload of clean linens.

"It's a girl, I feel the kinship clear to my bones. I do get to be called Auntie even though I'm a cousin?"

"Yes. Is Lantree speaking with Mr. Smythe?"

"Oh, well, no…I believe he forgot him in the rush to sterilize things."

"I'm going back down." Rebecca waddled toward the door. "It's hardly right to ignore Mr. Smythe when he's come all this way."

Melinda walked beside her, clearly ready to assist if she became overcome by a contraction. Rebecca was fairly confident that it was not going to happen.

"If we hurry we might not miss what he has to say," Melinda said.

Under her cousin's watchful eye, she reached the bottom step.

Mr. Smythe was alone in the room, sitting on the couch, his head nodding sleepily.

"I don't think we missed a thing," Rebecca murmured, feeling relieved.

Lantree burst into the room with an apron full of shiny instruments.

"What are you doing downstairs?" he said.

He took her elbow as though he believed he could hustle her right back up.

All of a sudden Mr. Smythe stood.

"Mr. Walker, I've come on a matter of great importance."

"Not now," Lantree said, hustling her back toward the stairs.

"It's concerning your brother, Boone Walker."

Lantree released her elbow and spun toward Smythe.

"My—"

"Brother?" Rebecca supplied, because it seemed that her husband had suddenly forgotten how to string words together.

"Boone," Melinda added helpfully.

"What do you know about him?" Lantree's full attention shifted from her to Smythe.

"That he was arrested, tried and found guilty."

Glum silence weighted the room. This was the worst possible news delivered at the worst possible time.

Not much could make this moment more alarming. Except for the gush of warm liquid dripping down her legs.

Lantree sat down hard on his chair and motioned for her to sit beside him. She shook her head. The last thing she was going to do right now was move from this spot and reveal the puddle.

"I was at the trial," Smythe said. "So I'm compelled to say that there was some injustice done to your brother."

"He did commit the crime," Lantree pointed out.

"Such as it was." Mr. Smythe lifted his chin,

squared his shoulders and stood as tall as his small frame would allow. "Mr. Walker, I'm a lawyer, new to the practice I'll admit, but with your backing, I'd like to represent your brother, get his verdict overturned."

"Why?" Lantree asked at the very instant a cramp made her half-dizzy.

She thought that the lawyer's answer had to do with wanting to make a name for himself, although it was hard to know for sure since her hearing had gone momentarily fuzzy.

Since she could postpone this no longer, she lifted her skirt.

"My water broke."

Lantree bounded up from his chair. "See to Mr. Smythe, will you, Melinda?"

He swept Rebecca up in his arms for the second time this morning and carried her up the stairs like she, in her large condition, weighed no more than a sack of flour. By the saints, she'd never get used to his amazing strength.

Closing the bedroom door behind her with his foot, he lay her down on the bed then helped her out of her clothes and into her birthing gown.

"I think it's time," she gasped.

He checked her. "Not quite, love."

"But it must be!"

He shook his head, grinning. "But everything looks as it should."

"In that case, I'm thirsty."

"I'll send Melinda up while I finish with the lawyer." He kissed her forehead. "I'll be right back."

Melinda brought up tea.

"What a pretty day to be born," her cousin announced, twirling into the room and setting the tray on the bedside table.

She sat down on the mattress beside her, smiling and clearly excited over everything that was going on.

"In the event that it does happen today. I feel like my insides are coming out and all my doctor says is 'not yet'…and then he grins."

"Well, he is a man."

"And if he weren't I wouldn't be—" she had to stop speaking and concentrate on a wave of pain "—doing this."

She began to shiver and feel sick to her stomach. Surely things were changing now.

She hadn't noticed Lantree come into the room, but he was stroking her hair and saying something that made no sense to her because her concentration was focused on riding a contraction.

"Only another hour, is my guess."

"Only! Are you insane?"

"Could be sooner. I love you, Becca. You are doing a wonderful job."

"Well, I resign…I…I need to push."

"Let me check again and see if it's time."

After a moment, his head popped up from between her spread knees. He was grinning even broader than before.

"I'm going to, no matter what—"

"Go ahead, Becca. Bring our baby into the world."

And so she did.

An hour later her baby girl, her pink and pretty miracle, suckled at her breast.

Rebecca drifted in a haze of contentment then woke up with a start near sunset.

Where was her daughter? Had she fallen asleep while suckling the baby? Had her baby slipped off the bed?

But no, there she was, cradled in her papa's big arms while he strolled about the room humming a soft tune.

She drifted off again then woke with Lantree lying on the bed beside her, still holding the baby.

"I'm in love." She sighed.

"Me, too."

"I've never seen someone so beautiful." And she truly had not.

"She looks like us both, I reckon, with those long fingers and toes."

"I see her being very tall…and lovely," she murmured.

"Like her mother."

"I love you, Caroline Rose," she said at the very same time Lantree said the same thing.

They laughed. Then, leaning across their sleeping infant, they kissed…long, slow and with a lifetime of joy arching between them.

* * * * *

MILLS & BOON®

The Thirty List

At thirty, Rachel has slid down every ladder she has ever climbed. Jobless, broke and ditched by her husband, she has to move in with grumpy Patrick and his four-year-old son.

Patrick is also getting divorced, so to cheer themselves up the two decide to draw up bucket lists. Soon they are learning to tango, abseiling, trying stand-up comedy and more. But, as she gets closer to Patrick, Rachel wonders if their relationship is too good to be true…

**Order yours today at
www.millsandboon.co.uk/Thethirtylist**

MILLS & BOON®

HISTORICAL

AWAKEN THE ROMANCE OF THE PAST